Hedgehogs in the Closet

BY JOAN CARRIS

ILLUSTRATED BY CAROL NEWSOM

J. B. LIPPINCOTT   NEW YORK

Author's Note: Although Baggsley-on-Thames is a fictional town, it represents all the wonderful small towns dotted across the English countryside. Other locations in the story are actual places.

I am indebted to several people who verified the accuracy of this story. Warmest thanks to Jan Bradley, Dorothy Duhig, Pat Baylis, John and Dorothy Meggitt.

Hedgehogs in the Closet

Text copyright © 1988 by Joan Carris
Illustrations copyright © 1988 by Carol Newsom

Library of Congress Cataloging-in-Publication Data
Carris, Joan Davenport.
  Hedgehogs in the closet.

  Summary: Unhappy with his family's move to England, eleven-year-old Nick slowly begins to thrive in the very British setting of his new home and school.   [1. Moving, Household—Fiction.   2. England—Fiction.   3. Schools—Fiction]
I. Newsom, Carol, ill. II. Title.
PZ7.C2347He 1988   [Fic]   87-45309
ISBN 0-397-32233-X
ISBN 0-397-32234-8 (lib. bdg.)

For my husband, who took us to live in England

1

Nick studied the small blue book that was his passport. His own face stared back at him, eyes and mouth solemn.

Marty peered over Nick's shoulder. "Hey, remember that movie, *Revenge of the Nerds*? You look like the Head Nerd."

Nick grabbed Marty's passport. "Well, you look about nine!" he retorted after a brief glance.

Marty jerked his passport away and turned to look back over the airplane seat at his parents. "I'm getting a new passport today at the U.S. Embassy in London, okay?"

"Not okay," his dad said. "That passport is for five years, mine's for ten—and we're both stuck with them."

"I'll have this thing till I'm nineteen!" Marty exploded. "It won't look anything like me then!"

"It's supposed to be a mark of distinction to have the worst passport picture," Mrs. Howard said. "I've heard that Americans living abroad compare pictures at parties."

I'll win *those* contests, Nick thought gloomily.

"Use mine, Marty," said Gus. He had been bending his passport to and fro, and it already appeared travel worn. He stood up between his parents and held out his booklet.

"Thanks," Marty said, "but looking nine's better than looking six. Anyway, you don't wear glasses. Nobody would believe that your picture is me." He shoved the passport into his pocket and slumped down in his seat beside Nick.

Who cares about a dumb old picture? Nick thought. All he wanted was to go back home where his friends were. But nobody in the family was listening. Since his birthday, a month ago, everything had been mixed up.

Nick remembered every minute of the steamy July day on which he had turned eleven. On that day, his guinea pig—Gooney Pig—had died of old age. Nick and Gus had buried him in their pet cemetery at the back of their yard.

2

That same day, Nick had had to separate all of his things—every single book, pencil, model car, and T-shirt—into three piles. Pile One was for storage in the United States, because the Howards had rented out their house. Pile Two would be part of the sea shipment sent to their new home. Pile Three had to be small enough to fit into two suitcases. Until the sea shipment arrived, those two suitcases were all Nick would have to call his own. The Howards were moving to England.

Nick didn't want to move. He had a hundred reasons why they should not go.

"I won't know anybody there," he had told his parents.

"You'll have a neighborhood with kids and a class with more kids," his mother had said. "Just like here."

"It won't be just like here! They won't be Americans!"

His dad had smiled. "That's right, and it's one reason we're going. You know the main reason."

The main reason was his dad's business. "I don't see why we have to be punished just because of your work!"

Mrs. Howard laughed. "Moving to England

should be easy, Nick. It's not like moving to France or Germany and having to learn a new language. Anyway, we're all addicted to things like food and clothing. For now, our income and job are in England . . . and we're a family, so we stay together."

"We did fine the other time Dad was overseas, remember?"

Mr. Howard stood up. "You managed beautifully. But it was tough, and it was only for a few weeks. Nick, you're just grasping at straws because you don't know what's coming and it's scary. Well, Mom and I are nervous, too, but we think we'll gain much more by moving than we're giving up. It's only for a couple years . . . and I know from experience that England's a terrific place."

And now here Nick was in an airplane seat on the way to England. He was not sitting next to his oldest brother, Jut. That would have been comfortable.

Instead, he had watched Jut become a tiny figure in the distance as their plane taxied down the runway at the Cincinnati airport. His mother had cried, and Nick thought he had heard his dad sniff in a suspicious manner. But Jut was a high school senior now. He was staying behind for his last year at Hampshire High. He'd be with them at Christmas, and all summer, but it wouldn't be the same. Moving without Jut was what bothered Nick the most. If only *he* could have moved in with Jut's friend and his family, Nick thought.

During the brief flight to Washington, D.C., Nick munched his peanuts and drank his Coke in silence. While he sat there, his whole life was changing. He didn't feel like himself anymore.

"Trying out for Mummy of the Month?" Marty asked. Nick pretended not to hear.

By the time they landed in Washington, Nick had had two soft drinks and munched his way through three bags of peanuts. No movie, of course, because the flight was too short, but there'd be a movie and two meals as they crossed the Atlantic.

Shortly after takeoff for England, the pilot explained that they would fly north first, along the American coast up to Greenland, where they would cross the ocean to Ireland, then down into London. That way, their time over water would be as brief as possible.

"Best news I've heard today," Mrs. Howard

said to the family. "I would love to have interviewed the pilot before we left Washington—just to make sure we have an old pro driving this thing."

Marty poked Nick. "*Howardus femalis nervosis*—your basic white-knuckled flier," he said with a grin.

Surprised, Nick smiled back. Usually, Marty shared his jokes only with Jut.

"Do you smell food, Marty?" Nick was more interested in food than any of his brothers. He was taller and bigger boned than either Jut or Marty had been at eleven. He never passed through the kitchen without eating something. "Look at these cool little dishes," he said when the trays arrived.

In spite of how he felt about moving and leaving Jut behind, Nick found that he loved flying. During the James Bond movie he drank Coke and ate more peanuts, and it was all free. He could have as much as he wanted.

After the film, the crew served a snack of biscuits (which his dad said were called scones), strawberry jam, and something beige in a small cup. "What's that?" Nick asked.

"That's clotted cream, luv," the stewardess said.

"Jam and cream on scones, mmm. Proper snack, that is. Luv-ly."

As she continued down the aisle, Nick noticed that Marty was staring. "I sure do like that accent," Marty said.

"You're not looking at her accent."

"Yes I am," Marty said. "And it's awesome. I wish I were going to an English school like you are."

Nick closed his eyes and leaned back against his seat. Marty was hopeless. Couldn't he imagine all the problems Nick would have in an English school? The awful possibilities had kept Nick awake many nights. Even though he wasn't hungry, Nick sat up and spread his scones with jam and clotted cream. "Mmhm," he said, mouth clogged. "Delishush!"

Northwest of London's Heathrow Airport, the plane ran into turbulent weather. Mrs. Howard retrieved Gus from the bathroom and made him sit between her and Mr. Howard with his seat belt buckled.

"I hafta go to the baaathroom!" Gus's voice reached everyone within a twenty-seat radius.

"Sssh! You've been in there every ten minutes, and you can't possibly have to go again."

The plane pitched sideways, then plummeted downward. It yawed to the right, then to the left, and dropped again.

"Oooo," Gus crowed with delight.

"How much farther is it to Heathrow?" Mrs. Howard asked.

"My stomach feels weird," Nick said.

Marty leaned forward to the map pocket. "Here, use the barf bag. Don't get any of it on me, and I mean it."

Nick opened the white bag and peered down into its plastic-lined interior. He had eaten his way across the Atlantic. All that stuff would never fit into this small bag. He closed his eyes and swallowed several times, taking deep breaths. I will not do it, he told himself, I will not.

As quickly as the turbulence had come, it left. Nick decided he could put the white bag back in its pocket. Overhead, the FASTEN SEAT BELTS sign stayed on as the plane descended to Heathrow Airport.

"I still hafta go!" Gus sang out.

2

The inside of Heathrow Airport astounded Nick. He had never seen so many different kinds of people and clothing—certainly not in Hampshire, Ohio.

Another planeload of people bustled past them, hurrying into the airport under a sign that said U.K. AND E.E.C. PASSPORTS ONLY. The Howards stood in a long line under a sign saying ALL OTHERS. Their line inched forward. People yawned, sighed, and shuffled their feet.

"Why's our line so slow?" Nick asked his dad.

"We don't belong to the European Economic Community, so they have to check our passports.

We're foreigners."

"I'm not a foreigner! I'm an American!" Nick said.

Behind them, a white-turbaned gentleman laughed softly and spoke to his companion in a language Nick had never heard.

Mr. Howard put his arm around Nick's shoulders. "In this country, kiddo, we are foreigners."

Nick checked out the people in their line. Many were in American clothing, but others were not. He eyed the floor-length dresses made of delicate fabrics adorned with gold. They reminded him of curtains draped to fit. He saw men in white turbans and funny clothes. Even their shoes were strange. Women and girls with colored dots on their foreheads had probably come from India, he thought, or somewhere in the East. Now *they* were foreigners.

At the passport control desk, Mr. Howard submitted all five of their passports plus his working permit that allowed him to live and work in England. When the official had stamped each passport, he said, "Remember that all expatriates must register with the police where they live. Do that straight away, please. Welcome to the U.K. Next?"

11

Frowning, Nick followed his dad. Register with the police? "This country has some nerve!" he announced.

"Why do they call England the U.K.?" asked Marty.

"It means United Kingdom. I'll explain in the car, okay? First, we have to grab two carts." Mr. Howard jogged toward the baggage area and everyone pelted after him.

When all ten of their bags had been loaded onto carts, Mr. Howard said, "Now we go through Customs. We have nothing to declare, so we go through the green doorway." They pushed their carts through the doorway, then sharply right past several tables and people in uniform.

Gus pointed to a group of officials and a pile of suitcases spread open on a table. "Why're they doing that? They're messing that guy's stuff all up!"

"Want me to tape their mouths shut?" Marty asked as he glared first at Gus, then at Nick.

"Want me to rearrange your face?" Nick poised his fist near Marty's chin. Marty had always linked him to Gus, treating them both as babies.

"Lower your voices!" said Mr. Howard. "You can't just waltz into a country and start criticizing." He sighed and rubbed his hand across his forehead. "They're probably opening that man's luggage because they suspect he's bringing somethng illegal into the country. It's for everyone's protection. Now no more questions till we get in the car."

In the car he'd rented for their first few weeks, Mr. Howard tensely gripped the wheel. It was on the right-hand side, where Mrs. Howard normally sat. "Okay, guys, it's easy to drive on the left, instead of on the right like at home, but I need silence."

"But I have a question," Gus wailed. "You said we could ask questions in the car."

"Well I lied!" roared Mr. Howard. "I forgot this part!"

Mrs. Howard held up her hand. "Peace. Look, kids, I am too young to die. I want your father to concentrate only on driving. Everything's the reverse of how we do it at home, remember? Just let him think, and let me read the map. We'll be in Baggsley-on-Thames before you know it. It's barely twenty miles."

In the backseat, Gus shoved his watch under Nick's nose. Proud of his new skill, Gus frequently announced the time. In a loud stage whisper he asked, "Why's it dark here? It's only six o'clock."

"QUIET!"

Nick put his mouth right against Gus's ear. "England is five hours later, so it's eleven o'clock here. Don't say any more or Dad'll kill us." Then he leaned back and looked out the window as Mr. Howard navigated the English car out of the English airport.

Baggsley-on-Thames, Nick thought. There were no town names like that in America as far as he knew. Only in England. Their tiny Windsor suburb was "in the very shadow of Windsor Castle," Mrs. Howard had said. She loved history. Nick hated it. History was like stewed tomatoes or liver. He was sure England was stuffed with history.

"It's all coming back to me," Mr. Howard said in a normal tone of voice. They were traveling in the far left lane hugging the shoulder of the road. Other cars winged past on the right at more than double their speed.

"Man, do they *drive* here!" Marty watched a red Jaguar disappear into the night.

"The limit on motorways or dual carriageways like this is seventy. They're talking about raising it to eighty since no one pays much attention to the limit anyway," Mr. Howard said.

"That's insane!" squeaked Mrs. Howard.

"*I'm* not surprised," Nick said. "This is a very foreign country." He looked over at Marty, who nodded agreement.

"Dual carriageways?" Marty whispered over Gus's head between them.

For a time no one said anything until Mr. Howard pointed out the dark bulk of Windsor Castle looming ahead of them. "There it is. Magnificent thing." He turned to grin at Mrs. Howard. "Think you can stand to see that every day of your life for the next couple years, honey?"

"Oooh," Mrs. Howard breathed, speechless with pleasure.

Big deal, Nick thought. He couldn't understand why adults went all twittery over buildings. Now if real knights were still jousting in the courtyard, that would be exciting.

Gus was asleep when they drove into the village named Baggsley-on-Thames. He missed the two short streets lined with shops, the post office, small inn, and tea shop that formed their new downtown.

"That's *it*?" exclaimed Marty.

15

"Windsor's just across the Thames River—practically next door—and it's much, much bigger," Mr. Howard replied. "You haven't seen our train station yet or the local schools. They're over a few blocks."

Nick and Marty exchanged bleak glances.

"Here we are—Kings' Ride!" Mr. Howard announced as he turned left onto a road lined with trees and houses.

Even in the dark, the differences between here and home were obvious. Instead of having a flat, open yard, each house was surrounded by tall, protective hedges and shrubs. Each house had a name—Berrymead, Ramsey Dale, Fareham. Where lights could be seen through the dense shrubbery, they glowed behind windows made of many tiny panes.

At the end of the street, Mr. Howard turned right between more hedges into a long, circular driveway.

"We have the only thatched roof on Kings' Ride," Mr. Howard said, smiling at Mrs. Howard. "I saved that for a surprise. Otherwise, it's just as I described it."

"Oh, Hugh, I must be in heaven. It's just gorgeous!"

In the car's headlights, the white stucco house looked awfully big to Nick. He almost expected a butler to throw open the double wooden doors. It didn't feel like home. "What's so great about a thatched roof?" he asked.

"It's teddibly English, old chap," Marty said in a fake British accent.

Heatherhurst was the name lettered over their doorway.

3

A flood of Englishness washed over the Howard family in that first week. Everything seemed different.

Their furnished house had no basement and no furnace. Instead, it had a white box the size of a large doghouse that sat in one kitchen corner and was called the boiler. It heated water for radiators and hot-water taps.

The refrigerator tucked under a counter. "Uh-oh," Mrs. Howard said when she saw the size of it. She pointed to a sign on its tiny freezer compartment that read, "Remove ice tray to freeze package."

"Now, Rae," Mr. Howard said, "remember how much you like the thatched roof on this place."

Every breakfast, Mrs. Howard said, "Somebody get ready to catch the toast!" because the Spanish toaster hurled the pieces wildly upward in opposite directions.

The German washing machine took two hours to scrub one load of clothes. It would slosh the clothes around for a few seconds, then stop altogether. Slosh again, and stop.

"Do you suppose it's thinking about something?" Mr. Howard joked the first time they washed a load. Nick and Marty laughed. Their mother said their clothes would be little rags by the time that machine had finished with them.

They were allowed to drink water only from the cold tap in the kitchen. It was safe. All other water came from huge tanks that sat in the attic. Mrs. Howard felt sure that mice had been drowning in those tanks for two hundred years, ever since the house had been built. The family could bathe in it, she said, but not drink it.

On their third day in England, Mr. Howard went to work and everyone else went shopping in Windsor. They were in Marks and Spencer's, a store that sold nearly everything, when Nick found something else that was different—the language.

"You say this is a *dustbin*?" he asked the clerk as he pointed to a new wastebasket in his cart.

"It's a dustbin," she said, smiling. "And you have two school jumpers, two boxes of biscuits, some digestives, a bag of courgettes, trousers, and several pair of socks."

Nick looked at the two brown school sweaters, boxes of crackers and cookies, the zucchini squash, and the pants in his cart. "I guess socks are still socks, right?"

The young clerk laughed. "You Americans are so witty—and handsome. The girls in your school will fancy you, I'm sure."

Nick sighed heavily. "My headmaster said I have to wear *purple*. Boys *never* wear purple where I come from."

Nick could have lectured for hours on the hideousness of purple. Purple anything was vomitrocious.

The clerk nodded matter-of-factly. "Baggsley-Hume, then. Very fine school it is. Your jumpers are over by the plimsolls and trainers."

Nick looked up at her blankly.

"Oh, dear. Let's see. Over by the sports shoes— for tennis or jogging. Does that help?"

Nick said, "We call them tennies or sneakers."

"Good luck, then. Look for me if you need more help." And she was off to another part of the store.

Nick pushed his cart over to the stacks of richly purple sweaters and pale lavender shirts. He refused to touch them. Mrs. Howard had to select his two sweaters and five lavender shirts. Plus two purple school ties.

"That is the barfiest color I have—"

"Martin, if you say even one more word about Nick's uniform, I promise you'll live to regret it."

"Can we go home now? I'm bored," Gus said.

"We'll quit for today." Mrs. Howard turned her cart toward a checkout counter. "It's going to take hours just to sort this stuff out and put it all away. Nick, you found the groceries I forgot? And you have Gus's sweaters?"

"Yes, and I got gray school pants and black ones. They call them trousers. Why can't I wear gray or black sweaters to match the pants?"

His mother squeezed Nick's shoulder sympathetically. "I'll fix the zucchini just the way you like it tonight."

"It isn't zucchini. It's courgettes, I think. Or maybe digestives. They have different words for *everything*."

Mrs. Howard looked in his cart. "See this label? Digestives must be these round graham crackers."

In line at the checkout Nick waited, helpless, glaring at his English school uniform. No one at home would learn about it, not if he could help it.

The Howards and too many bulky bags rode the bus from Windsor back home to Baggsley-on-Thames. Arms and shoulders aching from the weight of their load, they walked the four blocks from the bus stop to their house.

"Mom," Marty said, "if you don't learn to drive on the left pretty soon, we'll have arms like gorillas. Mine have already stretched two inches!"

"We aren't used to walking or carrying things like the British, I know. But it gives us time to appreciate everyone's beautiful flowers." She turned the key in the house lock and they dropped their burdens in the front hall.

"Okay, everybody take a job. Nick, you put out our wonderful British bars of soap."

Nick distributed the soap, putting his on the ceramic shelf below his mirror. On his mirror a sign read DON'T DRINK THE WATER. Each bedroom had a sink and mirror. The toilet had its own tiny room, and the bathtub was in yet another room, with heated towel racks. Mr. Howard had already backed into a towel rack after his bath and yelled a forbidden word.

Nick liked his broad, old-fashioned sink. So far, it was the highlight of living in England. At home, his brothers were always using the sink when he wanted it.

"Here are your clothes, Nick. Please put the ties where you can find them. We don't want a frantic tie hunt every morning when school starts." Mrs. Howard went into Marty's room next, with a similar speech, then into Gus's room.

Purple ties and lavender shirts. Don't drink the water. No car. Lousy television with hardly any cartoons. No friendly neighbors like in Ohio. No baseball games on Holly Tree Court. No kids at all, except at a distance.

Nick stretched out on his bed and covered his face with a pillow. He couldn't go hunting up kids as if he were home. It wasn't the same here. He didn't even speak the same language.

I'm just going to stay like this, he thought. I'm not even going downstairs for meals. If I stay here long enough, they'll have to let me go home.

I could go to Aunt Martha's in Indianapolis. The memory of his two girl cousins, who were the squealing sort, made him shudder. But it would be better than here. The United Kingdom, or England, or whatever they called it, was the pits. The absolute pits.

"Hey, Nick?" Marty called from across the hall.

Nick didn't budge.

"Yo . . . Nick?" Marty's voice came closer. "Hey, what're you doing?"

Through the pillow, Nick heard Marty's footsteps come into his room and over to his bed. Then the pillow came off his face.

"Put it back," he growled.

Marty covered Nick's face with the pillow. Nick didn't hear anything more. After a time the ancient chair in one corner of his room squeaked, so he knew Marty hadn't left.

"It's dullsville here, isn't it?" Marty said.

Nick didn't even twitch an eyelid underneath his pillow.

"I . . . uh . . . I'm sorry about what I said. But your whole school wears the same stuff. I'll bet some other guys hate purple like you."

Nick lay still—granite from middle America. What Marty was saying made no difference.

Marty could ignore everything British because *he* was going to an international high school, where many kids would be Americans. Their parents were working overseas the same as Mr. Howard. Marty's school subjects would be like those in Ohio high schools. He would wear decent sport coats and shirts to school. Even though his school was many towns away, his whole world wasn't changing the way Nick's was.

Marty shifted in the chair and it creaked alarmingly. "Look, Nick, I know how you feel. But it'll get better."

Nick wanted to yell HA! but of course he didn't. It occurred to him that his brother was behaving in a most un-Marty-like manner. If he hadn't known better, he'd have sworn it was Jut talking to him. The thought of Jut made Nick feel worse than ever and he squeezed back tears.

The chair groaned and then Nick could hear Marty's footsteps. "Stay there," Marty said. "Be right back."

Don't worry, Nick thought bitterly. I'm not going anywhere.

Marty was gone quite a while. Nick's stomach began to ask serious questions about food and he told it to shut up. If he died of starvation

25

there on his bed, they could sew him up in his sheets and bedspread, then slide his corpse down a plank like they did aboard ships at sea.

When Marty came back, he yanked the pillow off Nick's face again.

"Put it back!"

Marty sat down on the floor, on top of Nick's pillow. "I just talked to Dad," Marty said. "He's meeting us at Waterloo Station in London in an hour. At the bookstore in the middle. He said it was time we learned to use the trains so we could go anywhere we wanted."

Nick didn't move, but his stomach growled.

"I heard that! Dad's taking us to lunch, too. And he has a map of the tube—that's the subway—so we can go to the Tower of London or a movie or wherever we want. There's neat armor at the Tower, he said."

Nick felt the rock within him begin to crack. This was not Marty-from-Ohio. This was a different Marty.

"We're going to eat at Texas Lone Star. They have barbecued ribs and French fries, Dad said. *Real food.* Not Brussels sprouts or shepherd's pie or any of that garbage we've had in restaurants since we got here. Come on, Nick. If we miss the train, Dad'll think we can't handle it."

Nick didn't want his dad to think that. Besides, ribs and fries sounded terrific. What was left of his rock-hard determination crumbled. Today he'd go with Marty. He could starve to death tomorrow.

4

Training from Baggsley-on-Thames to Windsor, then into London, took only forty minutes. And it was simple. Whenever Nick or Marty had a question, people were eager to help.

Nick often didn't understand what they said. He sat in his train seat listening to the various accents. "Why don't they talk like English people on TV at home?" he asked Marty.

Marty frowned and whispered, "Don't be so loud. How should I know?" He pushed his glasses back into place. "But people in Boston talk funny. Not like us. Same with people from the South. It must be like that here, too."

Rats, Nick thought. He would never understand the kids in his school. He'd be asking "What'd you say?" all the time, and they would think he was an idiot.

Mr. Howard was waiting for them at London's Waterloo Station. He whisked them down the escalator and toward the underground trains. "Okay," he said, "study your tube maps and tell me what trains we should take from here to get to Gloucester Road Underground Station."

Later, seated at a table in the Texas Lone Star, they ordered barbecued ribs, chicken, French fries, and Cokes. Just like at home.

"You managed that trip like pros," Mr. Howard told them. "You'll handle this city in no time." He cleared his throat. "Now, let's not beat around the bush," he said.

Nick and Marty had to laugh. Their dad always came right to the point—and he always warned people by saying "Let's not beat around the bush."

Mr. Howard grinned. "I guess I'm pretty predictable. Anyway, I can see that you guys are bored, but after school starts, you'll have as many friends here as you had at home."

"Ha!" Nick inserted.

His dad leaned forward, putting his hand over Nick's clenched fist. "To be fair, you have to give it more time. Give England a chance. For me."

Pulling the word from deep inside him, Nick said, "Okay."

A very Texas-looking waiter brought their food, and Nick concentrated on his ribs. He was still planning on starving tomorrow, but today he would give England a chance.

"I ran off this morning without checking our milk saucers. Did you find any visitors?" Mr. Howard asked.

"We forgot to check, too," Marty said.

"Keep watching. You'll see a hedgehog any day now," their dad promised. "Did Mom call the cattery? She said she'd check on Eleanore and the kittens today."

Marty nodded gloomily. "The lady at the cattery said we had to wait two weeks to see them— till they 'settle in,' she said. This quarantine idea is terrible, Dad."

"Not to the English. They don't have rabies anywhere on the island, and quarantine is their protection. Every single animal or bird that can transmit rabies is quarantined for six months and no exceptions."

"Licky is going to hate it," Nick said. He longed to pet Licky's satiny black fur and feel the cat's weight in his lap. For four years, Licky had been

Nick's favorite, just as Fishhead had been Gus's.

Mr. Howard pulled his coffee nearer and settled back in his chair. "Cats don't mind quarantine, especially if their families are together like ours. But old Pierpont would have hated it."

"No quarantine in dog heaven," Marty said philosophically.

For a moment, all three mourned the death of the family's fifteen-year-old basset hound.

"Map time, guys. Let's find the best route to where you're going. Where are you going, by the way?"

"A movie?" Nick suggested.

Mr. Howard groaned, but he didn't say anything.

Marty said, "We can see a movie anytime, Nick. Let's go to the Tower of London. Isn't that where everybody got their heads cut off?"

Mr. Howard brightened. "That's the place! And the London Dungeons are here somewhere, and Madame Tussaud's Wax Museum. It has dungeon scenes, too. Big city for torture."

Nick nodded. He felt exactly like a victim of torture. "Okay," he said, "but next time, we see a movie."

After agreeing to meet in Waterloo Station at

six o'clock, they separated. Nick studied his map of the tube again. They could take either the District line or the Circle line to get to the Tower of London.

They rode the District line, but in the wrong direction, toward Kew Gardens instead of the Tower. They got off, rode back toward the center of town and on out to the Tower on the bank of the Thames River.

The Tower was actually many towers connected by stone walls. Inside, a large man with an even larger voice—and dressed in an impressive red Beefeater costume and tall black hat—conducted a tour. He showed them where Anne Boleyn's head had been cut off by order of her husband, King Henry VIII. Nick examined the spot, just in case there were still any bloodstains.

The Beefeater pointed out the window of the Tower room where two young princes had been murdered. He showed them the step where Princess Elizabeth had sat when she refused to be locked in the Tower. That had been about 400 years ago. Nick liked the story, even if it was history.

When the tour was over, they went up the

steps of the White Tower to see the armor. Nick imagined himself inside a young prince's suit of armor. It looks terrific, he thought, but uncomfortable. How could I go to the bathroom wearing all that metal? What if I had a mosquito bite? Or poison ivy?

From the Tower, they headed for the London Dungeons. Nick's opinion of the Dungeons would have discouraged other visitors. "Just a tourist trap," he said scornfully. "I thought it'd be good and scary."

"If you'd been in that iron cage hanging from the ceiling or stretched on one of those racks, it would have been scary all right," Marty observed.

It was nearly seven o'clock when Nick, Marty, and their dad entered the house. Nick thought he might as well go to his room and begin starving. No point in waiting. He had done London— and it had been okay. Now only school was left. It was bound to be bad. So the sooner he went back home, the better.

"Nick, come help me do the zucchini right," Mrs. Howard called from the kitchen.

Nick paused, one foot on the bottom stair step.

His mother was fixing the squash especially for him. Oh well, he'd already shot the day with the ribs and fries. He could go on his hunger strike in the morning.

Just as Nick was turning out his light that night, Marty hustled into his room and shut the door behind him. "Look what I got! It was drinking our milk in the backyard. Isn't it neat?" Marty held out his hand.

The prickly little hedgehog in Marty's palm was still, its nose tucked under its rounded body hump. Nick touched the shiny spines tentatively. "Those're sharp!" He stroked the hedgehog, front to back, smoothing down the brown quills.

After a long time, the hedgehog began to open up, and its black, furry face emerged. It was a piglet face, with bright eyes, perky ears, and a tiny snout. The hedgehog looked around the room but didn't try to escape.

"It likes being petted," Nick said.

"Marty? Where are you?" It was Mrs. Howard, in the upstairs hall outside Nick's room.

"Just saying good-night to Nick," Marty called out. He opened Nick's closet and plopped the hedgehog into a dark corner. *"Eee!"* it shrieked in fear.

"I'll bring milk later," Marty whispered to Nick. "Just leave it there. It sounds scared, and I think they like dark places."

Marty scooted out into the hall. "Night, Mom," he said. "See you in the morning."

When the house was quiet, Marty came to Nick's room with milk, and they played with the hedgehog.

Nick watched the odd animal snuffling in the saucer of milk. "He's brave, not scared anymore, see?"

"Probably just stupid," Marty commented.

"He is not! You don't know anything about hedgehogs!"

"Okay, okay! At least *I found him.*"

Nick watched the hedgehog move slowly around the room. Its little snout twitched as it waddled along. "I'm going to name him Spike," Nick said, grinning. "Can he live in my closet, Marty? I'll make sure he has food. Please?"

Marty had been staring at his bare toes. "Hunh?" he said now.

Nick repeated what he had said, but he could tell Marty wasn't really listening. "What's the matter?" Nick said after a bit. "Oh. You wanted him for yourself, didn't you?"

Marty stopped contemplating his toes and looked up. "No, he's yours." He sighed. "I was just thinking about school. I sure hope it isn't as hard as everybody says. If this school messes up my chance of a good class rank, I'm going to be really ticked off."

Nick stopped petting Spike and looked at his brother. Marty had actually talked to him about something important. "Who said it was so hard?" he asked.

"Some of the teachers back home. They have friends who've been teachers in international schools like the one I'm going to. They ought to know."

"But you're plenty smart!"

"Yeah, in Ohio. But maybe not over here."

"Think about me! English kids! An English school!"

Marty reached out and picked up Spike. "Yeah, Nick, but you'll be sort of a guest in your class. The American Kid. They won't expect you to know everything right off."

Nick wanted to believe him, but he couldn't. It wasn't going to be that simple. And Nick didn't want any part of it. He was going home. Marty could have Spike when he left.

"We'll keep him in your closet," Marty said, yawning. "I've got to sack out. Here, Nick, he can sleep on this pile of dirty clothes till you make him a nest of papers."

Marty shut the closet door. "I'll get one of my own," he said. "And one for Gus." He spread his arms grandly. "A hedgehog in every closet!" he promised, grinning.

"You sure about Gus?"

"He won't tell. We'll threaten him." Marty held out an empty palm and Nick slapped it, sealing the pact of secrecy.

Still yawning, Marty went off to bed. Nick flopped into his own bed, put his hands under his head, and got ready to starve himself.

No breakfast, he resolved. Marty could take over his job as Head Toastcatcher.

5

"What do you mean you're not coming down for breakfast?" Mrs. Howard stood by Nick's bed. "I'm making French toast, now that your father's found some maple syrup. He went all over London for that syrup. Just for us."

Nick hardened his resolve. She was making him feel guilty. She rarely acted that way, but he hated it when she did. "I'm not hungry" was all he said.

Silence. Then she said, "Well, perhaps you'll change your mind by lunchtime."

By lunchtime, Nick had not changed his mind but he was horribly bored. He was also furious with Gus, who peered in the door every few minutes.

"He's still in his bed!" Gus hollered down the stairwell each time he left Nick's doorway.

Around noon, Marty came in. "Why are you doing this?"

"Did Mom send you?"

"No, I came because I wanted to. Now, why're you doing this?"

No harm in telling, Nick decided. They needed to understand why or else they wouldn't know to send him home. "I'm not eating till I get back to America," he told Marty.

"Aw, geez, Nick." Marty rubbed one hand back and forth across his forehead, as if he had a headache.

Nick said nothing, and eventually Marty turned and left the room. Nick's stomach screamed, "Food! Bring me food!" as Marty left. Of course, the message didn't get through.

Starving was miserable. He had heard that starving people passed out from hunger and weakness. He hadn't known about the pain that went before. How much painful time would elapse before *he* passed out and felt nothing?

To distract himself, Nick got Spike out of the closet and both of them hid under the covers. "I'll bet you're lonely, huh, Spike? Me too. I don't have any friends here either. But Marty's going to find more hedgehogs and we'll have parties for you guys, okay?" Spike blinked sleepily.

"Nick, what are you doing under the blanket?" It was his mother and she was right next to his bed.

Nick popped his head out of the covers. "Uh . . . my hangnail had a toenail. I mean, my toenail had a hangnail, and I was pulling it off. It's . . . it's fine now."

"I've told you and told you—"

"I know, Mom. Use the toenail clippers. But it was nothing, really." Just then, Spike opened his quills against Nick's leg. Nick edged away from the sharp spines.

"Night, Mom. I'm going to take a nap," Nick said, trying to sound groggy so that she would leave before Spike did something noticeable.

"Nick, we're going to Windsor to shop and have tea at the Chocolate House."

Nick's stomach lurched when it heard the words *Chocolate House.* Spike snuggled up to his leg again, and again Nick edged away from him. One more jab, he thought, and I'll be poked right out of bed.

"We all want you to come with us, Nick. It

won't be the same without you. And I know you're hungry by now."

"I'm going to take a nap," he repeated firmly.

His mother felt his forehead, then stood erect. She waited several seconds before she spoke. "Marty told me your reason for not eating, but I don't think this will solve your problem." She paused. "We'll be back by five or six. Please take any phone messages." She bent down and kissed him and left.

Nick put Spike back into the nest of papers he had made for him that morning while everyone else was at breakfast. Spike nestled down and didn't move.

Nick got back into bed. He curled up in a ball so his stomach wouldn't hurt as much. He thought about pizza and soda pop, chocolate cake and cold milk. He wondered if any of the milk in the hedgehog's bowl was left. He even thought about barbecued hedgehog. When he went to sleep, he dreamed about the school's-out picnic in June in Ohio.

A squeaking sound woke him up. His dad had pulled the old chair next to his bed and was sitting in it, waiting.

"Son," Mr. Howard said when he saw Nick's

41

eyes open, "I don't know exactly how you feel, but I can guess. Mom and I realize we've asked you to do a difficult thing. But you are giving up almost before you've begun.

"All I'm asking is that you give this home a chance. As gentlemen, we agreed you would do that, remember?"

Nick managed a tiny nod. "I gave it a chance already."

"Less than a week isn't a fair trial, Nick, and you know it. Give it till New Year's. Four months. If you're still miserable, we'll work something out."

"Dad, do you really *have* to do this? Couldn't somebody else in the company have moved over here?"

"I have to do it. You remember when I was here before, when you were seven? I was paving the way then for what I'm doing now—setting up my business in England, with customers all over Europe."

Mr. Howard ran a hand over his forehead, back and forth, the same gesture Marty uncon- sciously copied. "Nick, I know you hate lectures, but sometimes the hardest things we do are the best things we do. And we don't realize it until later." Unexpectedly, he smiled. "What number is that?"

"Lecture Number Three, I think. It's one of your favorites."

"Thank you. Now could we go eat dinner so I can tell everyone what a tough day I had?"

The first Monday in September, Nick put on the hideous lavender shirt and the deep-purple sweater and tie. Marty did his tie, because Nick had never tied one.

As Marty rammed the knot into place, Nick said, "At home—geez, Marty, watch it!—this is Labor Day. We'd be going on a picnic. Some picnic this isn't."

When Marty left, Nick studied himself in the mirror over his sink. At least his hair looked decent. He practiced a broad, friendly-looking smile. It was so hokey, he knew it would be the wrong thing to do.

But who could tell what the kids here would like or make fun of? At home, he knew. He knew how to make kids laugh—how to be one of them. He was good in sports, and the boys respected that. The girls said he was "cute." His teachers said he was "a bit hot-tempered, but fair-minded

43

and generous with his classmates."

Nick made himself leave the room and walk downstairs.

Gus was in the front hall. He was hopping down its length and yelling, "Hurry up, I'm gonna be la-a-a-te!" He had on the dark-brown sweater, a white shirt, brown pants like Bermuda shorts, and the brown jacket. He would be going to the Boadicea First School, which some people called "infant school." Nick and Marty had learned not to call it that around Gus, because he kicked them in the shins every time.

After Mr. Howard had gone to the train, everyone else got into their new car. "You boys help me to stay in the correct lane," their mother said. "I still get confused every time I have to turn right."

They parked outside Nick's school, and Marty said, "Give 'em hell, Nick."

Mrs. Howard raised her eyebrows, but for once she let it pass. "I'll walk you to your room," she offered.

Nick shook his head. "Nobody else's mom will do that. Didn't you say this was the oldest grade in Middle School?" He got out of the car. " 'Bye, see you at three."

"Give 'em hell!" Gus yelled out the car window.

"That will be enough of that!" Mrs. Howard said, as dozens of heads turned to stare at their car . . . and at Nick.

Red-faced, Nick hurried up the sidewalk through a field of purple sweaters and lavender dresses. He had never felt so conspicuous.

6

Baggsley-Hume County Middle School looked like any school in America—a low, rambling brick building surrounded by playgrounds. Room 11 was on the second floor, and the name above the door read MRS. POPE. Nick put his shoulders back, looked straight ahead, and walked into the room.

The din in the classroom was considerable. Mrs. Pope stood behind her desk, calmly sorting papers. Not knowing what to do, Nick lounged against the blackboard and tried to look cool.

"I've still got conkers in our freezer. Mum says they won't be any good after so long, but we

could try and see," said a tall boy to his shorter friend.

Conkers in the freezer?

Right in front of Nick, at one of seven large tables in the room, sat a girl. Most of her hair was brown, but her bangs glowed orange. She was painting her fingernails with white-out liquid, the same stuff Jut used to blot out typing errors.

"Hey, Diggery? You didn't tell Nigel, did you? That wally's a grass, you know. Tell on his own mum, he would!"

"Ah, naff off," Diggery replied. "I'm no grass."

Nick's mind spun. It was even worse than he had imagined. He might as well be in China.

A ruler began regular tapping on the desk up front. Mrs. Pope tapped until all heads turned in her direction and the talking dwindled. "I know how excited you are to be back in school," she began.

Groans mixed with laughter around the room.

"Nonetheless," she went on, "I expect you to sit down and behave like ladies and gentlemen. We have three new pupils, and you don't want them to think you are noisy or rude. Please, sit down and no more nattering."

Students pushed and shoved until they were sitting with friends. Nick took an empty seat at a table with other boys. The boy next to him was Indian, Nick thought, and very handsome. He was tall and looked strong, though now he seemed uneasy. He must be new too.

Mrs. Pope called the roll of her thirty-eight pupils. No wonder I feel lost, Nick thought. I've never been in a class this size.

"I'll give out your timetables," Mrs. Pope said. "I want each of you to stand up and introduce yourself. You've known each other for years, I realize, but our new pupils do *not* know you. We're fortunate this year to have two children from other countries. We can learn a lot from them, and they from us, I hope.

"Alison, would you start off, please? Tell us some interesting bits about you and your family—perhaps hobbies, what you do at weekends, that sort of thing."

One by one the students spoke. They didn't seem a bit giggly or embarrassed.

When Diggery stood up to speak, Nick saw smiles around the room. He could tell that he was a class favorite.

"I'm Diggery Holmes." He grinned and went

slightly pink under a mass of freckles. "Sometimes called Copper-Top." He ran a hand through his reddish-orange curls. "But some people have to dye theirs to get it to look this way, and mine's real." He grinned at the girl with orange bangs and white-out fingernails.

"Cor, Diggery," the girl said. " 'Ee'll sigh ennythin'," she said to another girl at her table.

Nick blinked. She sounded like Eliza Doolittle in *My Fair Lady*.

Diggery continued. "I've got two brothers, two sisters"—here he made a face—"and I play the clarinet. I'm in Scouts and I like conker fights and BMX racing. And"—he paused for effect—"I *grew an inch* during school holidays."

Nick laughed with the rest of the class. He admired any boy who could joke about his own lack of height.

The first new student to speak was a girl named Fiona. She had an accent Nick understood, dark-auburn hair, and huge blue eyes. Nick thought she was gorgeous. He wondered if she'd like to come to his house and meet Spike, who was now tame enough to beg for food.

The Indian boy stood up and said his name was Akbar Mahanti. "I have twelve years, almost thirteen," he said, "but my English is bad. My vocabulary is little. I must be at this school one year before I go to special school to study for university. I am from Delhi, in India. It is much more warm there than here." His uneasiness falling away, he smiled around the room.

The girls leaned forward and smiled back at Akbar. Akbar stood taller. "I have BMX, as well," he said, looking at Diggery, "and I play trombone. But I do not know conker fights. I hope to learn conker fights." He bowed slightly from the waist in the direction of the teacher and sat down.

If Nick could have run from the room then, he would have. He felt like a bug under a microscope as he forced himself to his feet.

"I'm Nicholas Howard. They call me Nick. I'm from Ohio, in America. I don't have a BMX, and I don't know about conker fights either." He swallowed. "I must be a really boring person."

The class erupted into laughter. Two people clapped. Nick relaxed somewhat.

"I don't even play an instrument," he said, looking at Diggery, then at Akbar.

Again the class laughed, and Mrs. Pope smiled. "Tell us about your family and what you like to do," she urged.

"Well, I have two older brothers and one younger brother, Gus. We all like baseball and football and"—here he had an inspiration—"I'd like to learn rugby. Maybe somebody could teach me to play rugby."

"Excellent!"

"Eggie!"

"You teach us American football!"

The ruler began tapping the desk again, and the noise subsided. Nick dropped gratefully into his chair.

While Mrs. Pope passed out textbooks, Nick and Akbar compared timetables. Akbar had two classes of music each week, but otherwise they were alike.

Nick stewed over some of the classes entered for various days. French? He didn't know any French. And Creative Writing? For a whole hour twice a week? Poetry and Drama occupied other time slots.

"Man, am I in trouble," Nick murmured, eyeing his timetable. He dreaded the months ahead. Turning to Akbar he said, "Do you know French, too?"

"No. I shall learn. My father says it is simple. Not like English."

"Simple?" Nick decided that Akbar was a genius. Going to learn French just like that. No sweat.

"You will see," Akbar promised. He tapped his timetable with one long finger. "Here. This is bad. What is this 'Drama'?"

"You've got me. This isn't like my schedule in America. Not even close." That was not quite true, because English and Reading, Science, Math, Art and Physical Training were also on the schedule. But for now, he was worried about the strange things. *Poetry?* Barf.

Still, the rest of the morning was much like any morning in school. Mrs. Pope spoke the same brand of English that Nick had heard on television. She used several strange words, but he didn't have to ask their meanings.

"Excuse me, please," Akbar would say. "What does that word *reckon* mean?"

"Excuse me, please. What is a *full stop* which you want us to write?"

"Pardon, Mrs. Pope. I do not understand *harassing*. What is harassing?"

Nick leaned back in his chair and watched the long arm shoot upward as Akbar pursued his conquest of English . . . and saved Nick in the bargain.

At noontime, Mrs. Pope asked Diggery to show the newcomers to the gym, which doubled as the school's cafeteria. The four sat down together. Fiona and Diggery began eating.

Nick and Akbar looked at their plates, then at each other. "Is it a short hot dog?" Nick asked Akbar, who shrugged his shoulders.

Diggery leaned forward. "Trouble, mate?"

Nick pointed to the two rolls of dough on his plate.

"Toad-in-the-Hole," Diggery explained. "It's good."

"Luv-ly!" Fiona said—to Akbar, not to Nick.

Nick picked up one Toad-in-the-Hole and took a large bite. It was not luv-ly, it was dreadful. It was some kind of cold, greasy sausage in cold, heavy dough. He swallowed the bite as soon as it would go down. This food was well named, he thought. Probably tasted a lot like an actual toad.

On his right, Akbar chewed steadily, no expression on his face whatsoever.

"Does your family have a swimming pool?" Diggery asked Nick. "And lots of cars?" He grinned. "That's what we always see on the telly."

"Well, no, I mean no pool. We had two cars in America, but not here. Dad says if Ohio had trains like England, nobody'd have to have two cars."

"*No trains?*" Diggery and Fiona chorused. "That'd be bloody awful," Diggery added.

"What movie stars do you know?" Fiona asked. "Do you go to Hollywood often?"

Much as he wanted to impress her, Nick told the truth. "I don't know anybody in movies. Ohio doesn't have movie stars, and we'd have to drive for days to get to Hollywood."

"Oh. Saw-ree." Fiona turned to smile at Akbar.

Diggery scraped his pudding bowl for the last drop. "Hurry up, mates. Games outside, you know. We'll play rugby if you like, Nick."

Nick finished his lettuce salad and the dessert, which was a gummy white pudding. Tomorrow he would bring his own lunch. And he would warn the family about Toad-in-the-Hole.

7

Dear Jut,

Mom said she's written you lots, but I can tell more interesting things. Gus and I are in school now, and Marty starts in two days. He's bored and wishes you were here, too.

Are you seeing all my full stops? That's what they call periods. My teacher Mrs. Pope is ape over periods. And are you seeing all this real ink? All the really good schools use ink and ink pens like this, she says. It doesn't show much on my purple sweaters or black pants, but you can sure see it on the lavender shirts and the gray pants. But I have to keep practicing because I'm the worst in the

56

class. You wouldn't believe how beautiful every kid can write. The *first time* they write something it looks better than my stuff. Then they put lined paper under a new paper and copy it over! Every line is just so. They print, they don't use cursive. We use colored pencils to illustrate each paper with pictures. Mine stink.

I am coming home after Christmas. I promised Dad to try it for a while first. It's better than it was, but it still rots. Bobby said he was going to write and he hasn't. When you see him, give him a dead-arm from me.

The school food is barfy. Today we had chicken dustbins for lunch. It's pastry shaped like little wastebaskets with chicken glop inside. Mom only lets me carry lunch every other day. I am getting to like the desserts, and we get great candy here in Baggsley at the newsagent. It's a little store that sells newspapers and magazines and some groceries. We always have fresh pineapple that's really ripe. It comes from Africa. Other stuff comes from Israel and all over. Dad says looking in our fridge is a lesson in geography.

Rugby starts this week. It'll be rough—no pads. The games master—that's the gym teacher—says we have to wear gum shields. That must be what they call a mouth guard here. I'm going to play at school and Dad signed me up for the Baggsley team. They have games on weekends. It'll be messy because there's mud. You wouldn't believe the mud here. A neighbor lady came over and told us it didn't always rain like this. Nobody believes her. She didn't bring food or invite us to a party or anything like at home. Dad says that's the way here and be patient. Ha!

We had to pay money to the government for our TV—and color costs more than black and white. It's a license fee. Everybody pays it so we don't have those dumb commercials. We found a few funny shows like *The Two Ronnies* and *Smith and Jones*, but most of it rots. Mom and Dad love it. I was watching a cricket game till Dad said it was a test match and could be on for five days. I gave up. They have snooker on TV a lot. It's like pool only a bigger table. And they have dart matches. Dad's getting us a real English dart board.

The cattery finally let us see Eleanore and Fish-head and Licky. They were glad to see us, or maybe just glad about the leftover chicken we brought. They have a big cage in quarantine, taller than Mom, and wide. We can see them any-time now that they're settled in. I miss Licky but he didn't act real unhappy. We were locked in with the cats. Mom said it gave her the heebie-jeebies to be caged like that with 3 cats and 3 kids.

Mom likes it here. She's been to Windsor Castle two times already, and all over London. She went to a ladies' meeting of Americans who live here and signed up for a bunch of trips to famous houses and museums. She's all excited.

Marty and I go anywhere we want on the trains. Dad likes that but it makes Mom nervous. She's worried about the IRA. Do you know about the IRA? They plant bombs all over—especially in train stations or big stores where there are lots of people. If we see a package or a briefcase or suit- case just sitting around, we're supposed to run far away. It might be a bomb. The IRA are Irish fight- ing other Irish and some English people. Mom is reading a book called *Trinity* so she can under- stand it. She says it's a religious war but I don't know. That sounds dumb.

Did Marty write about Spike and Pokey? They're our hedgehogs. Spike's bigger and lives in my closet, and Pokey lives in Marty's closet. Don't be a grass and tell the folks, okay? A grass is a nark. The hedgehogs are pretty friendly, but they sleep all day. Good thing, or Mom would probably find out. We all miss the cats. I can't sleep with Spike like I used to with Licky.

Some kids in my class are cool. Akbar is from

India and he's nice. Funny, too. Knowing him is like being friends with an encyclopedia. Diggery is from here and he's always friendly. I went to his house and rode his BMX. If I stayed here, and I'm not, I'd want a BMX. Pretty soon it'll be time for conker fights. Conkers are like our buckeyes. I don't know the game yet.

We didn't have any Labor Day because England doesn't have it. We don't have Halloween here either, which rots. Instead, they have Guy Fawkes Day with fireworks. They don't even have Thanksgiving! Christmas is supposed to be a big deal. Well, that's the interesting stuff, and I'm sick of this ink pen now. Just pretend the blobs are illustrations, okay? See you real soon.

Love,
Nick

P.S. They have Scouts here. Diggery keeps asking me to sign up, but I'm not sure.

8

Rugby practices began ahead of season in Baggsley-on-Thames, a town known for its fine teams. Nick and his dad left early for the first Sunday-morning practice so that Nick could meet the coach.

Wearing old shorts and a sweatshirt, as Diggery had told him to, Nick got into the car. He had washed his face and hair, but he felt it had been wasted effort. Everywhere he looked, water stood in muddy puddles. His legs were freezing in spite of new wool knee socks. He could guess what would happen to his new rugby shoes. "It can quit raining anytime," he said.

Mr. Howard huddled inside a raincoat, his

61

head tucked down into the wool muffler around his neck. "I don't think they pay any attention to a measly little rain like this. I'd guess mud and rugby are synonyms."

At the playing fields on the banks of the Thames River, the coach strode forward to meet them. "I remember you," he said briskly to Mr. Howard as they shook hands. He looked down at Nick. "And this must be the lad. He looks a good one. Do ye play rugby in America, then?" It was "rrroogbee" when he said it, with an *r* of unusual richness.

"No sir." For some reason he didn't understand, Nick added, "But I've played football."

"Och! American football. Sissy game," Coach Stewart said, winking first at Nick and then at Mr. Howard. "Rugby is for men. Have ye a gum shield?"

Nick pulled a grimy piece of plastic from his shorts pocket. His dad looked at it and shuddered.

"Right, then. I'll give you instructions as we go along. Learn as you play. Your mates will help." He glanced at his watch and turned to Mr. Howard. "You should return for him about twelve. They'll be fagged by then."

Nick met the group of eleven-year-olds first, about twenty boys who hoped to play regularly, including Diggery. Then he met the rugby ball. He tried tucking it under his arm like a football, but it was bigger around and its ends more gently curved. It had a good, solid feel, but it would be harder to hold on to.

"Now, lads," Coach Stewart began in a rousing voice, "we are beginning a virrrgin season. We have not lost a single game!"

Nick and Diggery glanced at each other and stifled their laughter.

"We have two new players," the coach went on, "one from South London"—here he pointed to a tall boy at Nick's left—"and an *American football player*." With a dramatic gesture he pointed to Nick. "We shall be invincible!"

All twenty boys cheered. Diggery pounded Nick so heartily on the back that Nick almost fell down.

The coach held up black shorts, socks, and a handsome red-and-black-striped jersey. "This is our new kit, which I'll give ye after practice. Take off any rings or watches, put in your gum shields, and we'll do laps round the field to warm up."

63

Nick slipped his gum shield into place. Real uniforms. He couldn't take his eyes off the black-and-crimson jersey. It was the coolest jersey he'd ever seen. Wait till Jut sees *that*, he thought.

The next two hours were the most foreign, the most physical, and the most exhilarating that Nick had ever lived. He did drop the ball, but not as often as he had feared.

"Meaner in the scrum, lads! Push with your heads and shoulders! Be agrrrressive!"

For a few relaxing minutes, they sat in the mud and listened to Coach Stewart's lecture on the scrum. The scrum, or scrummage, occurred after certain infringements, to determine which team would next get the ball. Heads and shoulders touching, arms around each other, the forwards of both teams stood in opposing triangles with the ball on the ground between them. The idea was to work the ball to the back of your scrum to one of your own players.

In two separate teams, the boys went into a scrum again. Nick and Diggery strained forward, grunting with effort, their bodies in a heaving crush with fourteen other bodies.

"Get yur bloody finger outa me eye!"

"Watch where yur grabbin'!"

Diggery inched his foot toward the ball, trying to worm it outside the scrum to the boy playing scrum half for their side. The ball scooted toward Nick, who got a toe on it and sent it out between a player's feet. Their scrum half grabbed it and began running.

"Well done!" Coach Stewart thumped Nick and Diggery on their backs.

They spent nearly an hour practicing passes.

"Dinna pass it for'ard!" the coach bellowed at Nick, his Scots accent broadening with excitement. "Off to the side, or behind ye! Yurr a natural passer, lad!"

At one point in the practice, the new boy from South London crashed into Diggery, who was much smaller. Diggery dropped like a stone. He was carried to the sideline by some father-spectators, who sat with him until he came around. Diggery waited a few minutes, then went back into practice.

"You okay?" Nick asked.

"No sweat!" Diggery grinned. "That's from an American movie. It's right, isn't it?" he asked.

"Yeah, it's right." They walked down to the end of the field where the group had gathered. "You know," Nick said, "I don't think my mom should see any rugby. She thinks football is rough."

"You mean soccer?" Diggery asked, looking confused.

"No, football."

"Soccer . . . is . . . football." Diggery emphasized each word.

"You mean they call soccer football here?"

"Soccer . . . *is* . . . football. Only you lot call the American football football! But you hold on to the ball, right? I've seen them do it on the telly. In soccer, you can only touch the ball with your feet. So it's *foot*ball, right?"

"I never thought of it that way before."

After practice, Mr. Howard was waiting in the parking lot. Nick wrenched open the car door, eager for any warm, dry place, eager to show off his cool new kit, as the coach had called his uniform. "Smashing!" was what Diggery had said.

"Hi, Nick . . . Good Lord!"

Nick took another look at himself. He was a little muddy. Good thing his uniform was still in a plastic bag.

"Don't get in!"

"It's freezing out here if you're just standing around!"

"Let me spread out the newspaper. I didn't want to read it anyway." Mr. Howard speedily upholstered the passenger side of the car with the *Sunday Telegraph.*

"Well, how was it?" Mr. Howard asked as they drove away. "Besides muddy, that is."

"The coach said I was a natural. He said I was 'boorrn to play rrroogbee'!" Nick said in perfect imitation.

His dad chuckled. "Born to play rugby, huh? Just what I thought after seeing your football games last year." He grew serious. "Don't take any crazy chances, son, okay? No glory plays . . . know what I mean? It's a game. Not worth breaking any bones. Your mother would never forgive me. We'd have to run away from home."

"She should never see a game, Dad. I mean *never.*"

"Anybody get hurt today?"

Nick explained how Diggery had been knocked out. "He came right back in, though. He's tough."

Mr. Howard was quiet. Then he said, "Why don't I fix up a good first-aid kit, just in case? I could be at all the games and most of the practices. After all, they went out of their way here to let you be part of the team. We ought to try to be as helpful as possible."

Nick's first impulse was to say No, don't bother, I'm not going to get involved. But the rugby kit was in his lap. And Christmas was three months away. Coach Stewart had said the season would not end till April.

They rode for several blocks. As they turned onto Kings' Ride, Nick said, "Yeah, maybe you could do that. Rugby's even rougher than football."

"Yes," his dad said, "these people are tough." He turned in their driveway and pulled into the narrow garage. "I can hardly wait to hear what your mother says when she sees you."

"But I was boorrn to play rrroogbee!"

"Uh, hunh, but I don't think she believes she was boorrn to be a laundrrress!"

That night Marty found another hedgehog in the back garden. Up in Nick's room, Marty said, "Let's give this one to Gus, okay?" The new hedgehog lay curled in a spiky ball on Nick's bed. It was tan colored, with a black-striped head and larger ears, like Marty's hedgehog.

"Gus *est le* blabbermouth," Nick said, looking

up from his French book. Mrs. Pope gave him such a proud smile every time he uttered a word in French that he was learning to enjoy it.

"C'est vrai," replied Marty, now in second-year French. "He is sometimes. But we'll threaten him. We all lose our pets if he blabs—so he'll be quiet."

Nick shrugged his shoulders. "Okay by *moi.*"

Gus had been asleep, but he woke up with enthusiasm when they put the hedgehog in his hands. Much closer to the stories of Beatrix Potter than either Nick or Marty, Gus said right away, "It's Mrs. Tiggy-Winkle!"

"Sssh! If the folks know you've got him—"

"It's a *her!* It's Mrs. Tiggy-Winkle!"

"Okay, okay! It's Mrs. Tiggy-Winkle, but she has to be a secret." Marty then produced his own Pokey, and Nick got Spike out of his closet. The new hedgehog uncurled on the floor and peered at its relatives. Soon, all three hedgehogs were in a clump snuffling one another. Spike talked to the newcomer in short, soft grunts.

Nick laughed. "He's telling her about the good food at this hotel."

He showed Gus how to pet his hedgehog. Marty explained how they saved food scraps and milk each night as they cleaned up the kitchen. "They don't eat much. Just leave a bit of everything on your plate and we'll put it in a napkin for you to take upstairs. Keep her hidden in your closet, and *don't tell the folks.*"

"I won't tell," Gus promised. He stroked Mrs. Tiggy-Winkle carefully, front to back. "We don't have show-and-tell here," he said regretfully.

"But your school's okay, isn't it?" Marty asked.

"Yeah." Gus put Mrs. Tiggy-Winkle in his lap. "We do plays and things. And write stories. Mrs. Cameron says I write real good stories."

"It runs in the family," Marty said. "You know, I'll bet I have to write even more here than I did in seventh grade. That was the year I thought my arm'd drop off."

"Yeah," Nick said, "but you said the kids are nice."

"They're better than that—they're great! Half the class is new, so everybody's looking for friends. And you should see the biology lab. It's totally awesome."

"Are all the kids Americans?"

"No way. We've got kids from twenty-six different countries. Maybe half are Americans like us. They all want to go to college in the States, so they have to have an American curriculum."

Marty picked up Pokey. Yawning with the sleepiness of Sunday night, he stood up. "Tons of homework, though. I'd better do my French, because I have a zillion pages to read in *Great Expectations*." He frowned. "Man, is that boring! Dickens got paid by the word, and you can tell he squeezed out as many as he could think of."

Marty went off to his desk, and Nick helped Gus hide Mrs. Tiggy-Winkle in his closet. "Make her a bed of paper, Gus, real soon. Way back in a corner where it's dark and Mom won't see her, okay?"

Gus nodded. "Night, Mrs. T," he crooned as they shut his closet door.

"Remember, she's a secret, Gus. If the folks find out, we'll have to let them all go."

In his own room, Nick set Spike on the bed next to the desk. "Spike," he said, "how'd you like to move to America with me in a few months?"

Spike hoisted his quills in the air and belched.

"Don't want to go, huh?" Nick picked him up and opened his closet door. "I don't blame you. Moving stinks."

Nick put the hedgehog in his nest and shut the closet door. Silently, he piled up Monday's schoolwork. Like Marty, he had more homework than in America. Maths, as he had learned to call it, was easy, because he was a bit farther ahead in mathematics than his class in England. The creative writing was killing him by inches. In poetry, they were reading about ships and the sea, which was okay. Drama, the class he and Akbar dreaded, had not yet begun.

9

Only a few days after the first rugby practice, there was another, late Wednesday afternoon. Nick wore the new uniform. He had cleaned his muddy cleats. His mother took a picture of him to send to the two sets of grandparents. "That uniform looks better now than it ever will again," she predicted.

The rest of the team was in full kit also. Mr. Howard asked if he could take a team picture. He volunteered to have the snapshots enlarged, one for each boy. A beaming Coach Stewart, chin up and chest thrust forward, stood in the center of the boys for the picture. "Big smile, lads!" he boomed. "We're going to be immorrrtalized!"

"This's brilliant!" Diggery told Nick. "We hardly ever have pictures."

Nick almost said, "We *always* have team pictures where I come from," but he bit the words back. His dad had warned them not to keep saying how things were done in America. "They'll ask if they want to know," he had said.

So Nick just nodded at Diggery and smiled while his dad took three pictures—to be safe.

The second practice was as brutal as the first, except there was no mud because it had miraculously failed to rain for three days. Without regular moisture, the sandy soil turned firm in a hurry. Nick missed the mud. It had cushioned his falls and let him slide rather than land with a jarring thud.

Even more miraculous, however, was that Diggery passed the ball to him near the end of the practice . . . and he didn't drop it. He fumbled the thing for an awful second or two before he got a grip on it. Then he tore down the field and across the goal line.

"Touch it to the grrround, Nicholas!"

Nick did as he was told. As on Sunday, he got pounded on the back by a delighted coach. "There's where you Americans get your touchdown!" he said. "The ball must touch the ground or it's no' a try. That was a fine try!"

"But I didn't just try. I did it, didn't I?"

"You scored a try. And it's worth four points."

Nick stared up at him, dying to say that *try* was a stupid name for it.

"And you're wanting to call it a touchdown, are ye?"

Slowly, Nick shook his head. "No, I guess we can call it a try."

At the end of the practice, Coach Stewart called the team together. "You'll be wanting to save your shirts and shorts for games," he said. "But I knew ye wouldna leave them home today!" He took a piece of paper from his pocket. "Our first game is Sunday fortnight. Then we wear the full kit. Go on now, lads, and do your homework."

Nick hopped into the car and sat on an old blanket his dad had spread out. "Did you see my try? Did you see it?"

Mr. Howard rubbed Nick's head as though he were a puppy. "Jolly well done, and all that! Good show!"

Nick said, "They call it a try, not a touchdown. But you have to touch the ball to the ground or it doesn't count. How did rugby and football and soccer get so mixed up?"

Mr. Howard steered the car out of the parking lot. "Probably the language barrier again. My favorite playwright, George Bernard Shaw, said that 'England and America are two countries separated by the same language.' "

"Smart man," Nick observed.

The following days were not at all like Nick's first days in England. At Diggery's insistence, and that of Nigel, whom he had come to know, Nick joined Scouts. The Boy Scouts were popular in England, he learned. Soon they were going on a hiking weekend in Wales—only three hours away by car. And there would be other weekend trips.

Nick hadn't planned to join, but Diggery wouldn't take no for an answer. I can't tell him I'm going home at New Year's, Nick thought. He'll think I don't like him or something.

Nick spent a Saturday at Diggery's house again. This time he rode the BMX on trails in Windsor Park. Diggery rode Nick's bike, which had finally come from America in the sea shipment with the rest of their belongings.

His class planned their Christmas entertainment, an elaborate medieval pageant in which Nick and Akbar were to be knights—in real armor. As the oldest class, the fourth-years were "expected to put on the best sketch," as Mrs. Pope had said. Her class always began preparing way ahead of time.

Each day hurried past, and Nick was caught up in the life . . . even though he was trying not to be. In bed at night, he listened to the train as it chuffed into Baggsley-on-Thames and out again. He woke to the same sound every morning. In his mind he could picture that train perfectly and recall its smell—a blend of damp wool, tobacco smoke, and ripe upholstery.

Right above his bed was the picture of the Baggsley Under-Twelves in their black-and-crimson jerseys. Their first game was only a few days away.

When a letter came from Jut, Nick fell upon it.

Hi, Nick, (*Jut began*),
Greetings from the colonies! I see some kids in your class around town, and they always tell me to say hello. I gave Bobby the dead-arm, just like you said. While he rubbed the sore place, he promised

to write. I wouldn't keep my finger in my eye waiting, know what I mean? Bobby's a nice kid, but not real mature.

Sorry I missed talking to you last time I called. The folks said you and Marty were in Windsor. Sounds pretty cool to me. All we've got is McDonald's—no castles or Chocolate Houses.

School's going great, and our football team's really tough this year. We beat Centerville, can you believe that? I'm doing the write-ups for the school paper, and when I interviewed the coach after the game, he was so excited he could hardly talk. Me, I'm waiting for basketball season!

Jason Markham said to say hi. I see him every time I'm at Gwen's house. I think she'll be a candidate for Homecoming Queen. If she is, I have to wear a suit as her escort, so warn the folks that I'll need money. I needed a suit anyhow.

Your letter was great. You guys have done so much over there compared to me. I think about it every time a letter comes, and I'm sure sorry I was a senior this year. Any other year and I'd have jumped at the chance. Keep a list of your favorite places, so you can show me when I come for Christmas. The principal said I could take extra days if I did homework in advance. I'll have almost a month that way!

I'm supposed to be working on college applications, so I have to sign off. I don't think you should come home, Nick. Living with another family is okay, but not terrific. And staying with Aunt Martha in Indianapolis is crazy! Why don't you make a list, like I did for colleges? List the good points about England and the good points about home— or Indianapolis (Good luck!). Then list the bad things for each. Let me know how it comes out, okay?

See you soon,

Jut

Nick reread the letter. It was as if Jut were with him while he was reading it. When he finished, Nick put the letter in a safe place in his desk.

Two nights later, when Mr. Howard got home from work, he came upstairs to Nick's room.

"Well, one more Saturday down the drain," he said. "They think I'm crazy in this country, working on a Saturday, but there's so much to do, I can't believe it." He sat down on the bed beside Nick, who was reading *Winnie-the-Pooh*. He always read *Winnie-the-Pooh* when he needed cheering up.

"Let's not beat around the bush," Mr. Howard began.

Good ol' Dad, Nick thought.

"I haven't said anything, or asked any questions, since we made our deal. You know Mom and I only want you to be happy. Now, nobody can be happy every minute. Life isn't like that. But we want you to feel secure and settled . . . and I need to hear from you how it's going."

"I miss being home."

"Of course! Homesickness is very real . . . and we all feel it. Mom and I would give anything right now to see our friends. And frankly, doing business over here is a lot harder." He stood up and jammed his hands into his pants pockets. "A *lot* harder," he repeated. "They do things so differently."

"That's for sure."

Mr. Howard paced over to Nick's window and stared out. "But maybe they're right. Just because we know, uh, what we think we know," he said vaguely, "doesn't mean we are right."

"Yeah, Dad?" Nick saw that his father needed to talk.

"Now *you*," Mr. Howard said, turning from

the window and pointing at Nick, "have been a good ambassador. But I don't know about me." He sat back down on the bed. "I haven't been so hot."

Nick closed his book. "What do you mean I've been a good ambassador?"

"I've seen it! I heard what Diggery said about the pictures and what a good idea it was. Now we always do that back home—don't think anything about it. If you'd said that, it would have been a putdown, like saying, 'Oh, we do things better in America.' But you didn't say a word! And you haven't argued with the coach. Heck, you always argued with your coach at home. And with your teachers.

"Mom says you've got real nice friends, and you joined Scouts. You're the best ambassador America could have sent."

Nick and his dad had never had a conversation like this. He didn't know what to say, though he felt good about being a wonderful ambassador. He hadn't even known he was one.

"Dad, you're the one who told us not to be saying how it was in America all the time."

His father groaned. "I know, I know. And if I said *This is how we do it in America* once today,

I said it a thousand times!" He leaped up off the bed again. "Today, I was the same 'ugly American' they wrote about in the book. You know, this is *so frustrating* . . . and it's really hard!"

Nick could not resist. "Sometimes, Dad, the hardest things we do are the best things we do."

Mr. Howard stood still. Gradually, his body relaxed and he smiled. "You know, Nick, this's the first time I've loosened up all day." He laughed softly. "Do you believe that now? Lecture Number Three?"

"I don't know. I don't know anything anymore."

"Nick, what's so much better at home?"

Nick pulled a paper from his pocket. "Jut said to make a list. At home are my friends, real food, football, my school, the quarry to swim in, everything I know."

"Have you been writing your friends?"

"Well . . . no."

"Why not?"

"They haven't written *me*! Not even Bobby! And I've been busy. We're already working on our Christmas play, and I've got Scouts and homework. . . ."

"And rugby," his dad added. "They're expect-

ing you to play scrum half tomorrow, for part of
the game at least. That's a real honor for some-
one who's only been playing the game three
weeks."

Nick looked down at his bed.

"It's natural homesickness, Nick. I can't expect you to understand that it will go away in
time. And you're stubborn, too. It's a family trait.
I wouldn't have my own business if I weren't
mule stubborn and determined to make a go of
it."

Nick folded up his list.

"I'll stick by what I said. If you still want to
go home after the Christmas holidays, we'll send
you back with Jut. We'll work it out somehow."
He paused. "But for now, we should try to enjoy
it here—not compare it to America all the time.
Me too!" He grinned ruefully.

Nick slid his book under the bed. "Sure, Dad."

"Hey, Nick, my closet stinks." Gus barged into
Nick's room without knocking. "It stinks pretty
bad."

"Well, Gus, we'll just have to examine it
and—"

"No, Dad, I can handle it!" Nick vaulted off
his bed. He could guess why Gus's closet was

83

smelly. "Show me your closet, Gus, okay?"

"I haven't seen Dad all day," Gus began.

"But you'll see him the rest of the weekend." Nick shooed Gus ahead of him. "See you downstairs, Dad, in just a minute."

10

Nick sniffed in Gus's closet. "Geez, Gus!" he said, backing away. "We told you to clean up after her!"

"I'm not touchin' that stuff!"

Nick bent down, putting his face level with Gus's. "Who do you think cleaned up after you when you were a baby?"

"Mom did. Moms like that stuff. Not *me*, boy!"

"Nobody likes that stuff. Clean up after her right now or Mom'll find out! Lucky for you she doesn't ever crawl way back in your closet!"

Gus stomped the carpet. "I don't know how!"

"Marty and I'll show you. Then you're on your own . . . or else! If Mom finds her, we'll all lose our pets."

Nick and a thoroughly irritated Marty helped

Gus to clean up after his hedgehog. "You need more papers, Gus. I told you that," Marty said. He got the Wild Orchid spray from the bathroom and doused Gus's closet as a final touch.

Gus hopped up and down while Marty sprayed. "All my clothes'll smell like that! Stop, stop!"

"Believe me, it's an improvement," Marty said grimly. "Come on, you guys. Dad bought a VCR today so we could see movies at home . . . where it's cheaper. If we don't show up for the movie, they'll come looking."

Nick and Marty went downstairs while Gus changed into his pajamas. Soon they were settled in the den, enjoying *Raiders of the Lost Ark* all over again.

"Hey, Nick, move over. And give me some blanket. It's freezing down here." Marty left the floor and snuggled into the blanket, the couch, and his brother.

"I wasn't smart enough to appreciate our basement at home, but at least it kept the first floor warm," Mrs. Howard said. She was on the other sofa, huddled under another blanket with Mr. Howard. "My legs are frozen up to the knee every day by noon. And it's only September!"

Gus, who wore a woolly one-piece sleeper,

hopped onto the couch beside his mother. "You're just not wearin' the right clothes. I'm warm."

Mr. Howard said, "I wonder what they'd think at the office if I turned up in a pale-blue blanket sleeper?"

"I'm sure we'll adjust," said Mrs. Howard, "and I know it's colder in the north of England."

"Switzerland, too, but it's drier there and that makes a tremendous difference. Henri said we could have their place for ten days in February, and I think we should go for it. That's a mighty generous offer."

"Awesome!" Marty exclaimed.

In February, Nick thought. After I'm gone.

"Where's Switzerland?" Gus asked.

"On the Continent," Mr. Howard replied. "East of France and south of Germany. It's mountains and snow and learning to ski, Gus. And we'll live in a chalet owned by a nice Swiss fellow in my office. We'll need lessons, but we're all good ages for learning to ski. Especially me!" He grinned.

"Everybody hush up," Mrs. Howard said. "We're coming to my favorite part of the movie."

For part of the rugby game on Sunday morning, Nick played scrum half for the Baggsley Under-Twelves. He wasn't spectacular, as Coach Stewart swore he would be, but he wasn't terrible either. He dropped the ball only twice.

"Verra good, lad," the coach told Nick at the end of the game. "We won. Canna ask for more than that."

The rest of Nick's week was crammed with school and homework and getting ready for the Scout trip to Wales. Diggery's mother lent Nick a Scout uniform that had belonged to Diggery's older brother. She told the Howards that she had an entire wardrobe full of scouting equipment and Nick could use whatever he needed.

The night before the trip, Mr. Howard brought home a new pup tent. "They call it a hike tent here," he told Nick. He and Nick practiced setting it up in the back garden so that Nick would look like a pro in Wales.

Friday, at two o'clock, the Scouts were excused from classes. Mr. Fowler, the Scoutmaster, wanted their camp set up well before dark. Thirty boys, most of their troop, were going to the Brecon Beacons, a mountainous region of Wales near England's western border.

Nick, Diggery, and Nigel stowed their tents

and gear in the back of the bus.

"Not a bus, you wally," Nigel said. "It's a coach!" He nudged Nick's duffel bag. "Any food in your rucksack?"

"Just clothes. Nobody told me to bring food."

"I've got digestives," Diggery volunteered. He reached into his rucksack for the packet of graham-cracker-like cookies. "Fowler never brings much to eat. He thinks we all want to look like him." He and Nigel hooted with laughter.

Just then the Scoutmaster stood up at the front of the coach. Tall and erect, Mr. Fowler was prison-camp thin. He was also white haired and persnickety. Diggery's mother had told the Howards, "He has his own way of doing things."

"Attention, lads!" The Scoutmaster read the names in each patrol. He read only last names. After attending just one meeting, Nick had learned to answer to Howard.

"Right, then," Mr. Fowler said, folding up his list of names. "This coach has no loo. If any Scout needs to pee, he should do it now, as we'll not stop. I mean to have a proper tea in camp." He checked his watch. "The coach leaves in five minutes sharp."

Nick jabbed Diggery in the ribs and whispered, "He said *pee*! Did you hear him?"

"Why're you whispering?"

Nick went right on whispering. "Because nobody's supposed to say that, that's why!"

Diggery handed Nick another digestive. "We say pee all the time. BBC radio as well." He patted Nick's arm as if he were a father. "There, lad, you'll get the hang of it here. Just stick with Diggery Holmes." His blue English eyes were gleeful as he crammed half a digestive into his mouth.

On the trip the Scouts told jokes and sang American songs like "Camptown Races"—to Nick's surprise. As the coach neared Wales, the country became more hilly. Gradually, the hills grew into low mountains, and everywhere Nick looked he saw rocks and sheep. He had never seen so many sheep, some all white, others with black faces.

They set up camp in a valley near a broad stream, with the mountainous Beacons all around them. Water gushed over a rock outcropping to join the stream below. The Scoutmaster ordered Woodpecker Patrol to help him set up the troop tent near a wooded area.

"All other patrols will set up their tents straight

away. Pheasants, hurry along now. You'll pre-
pare tea."

Nick was a Pheasant, like Diggery and Nigel.
All seven Pheasants hustled to set up their tents
and start a fire. As patrol leader, Diggery gave
orders. "Get the big teapot!" he hollered. "That
dark-blue one we hang over the fire! And tea
and bread and jam and milk!"

"This bloody stake won't go in! Doesn't it ever
rain 'ere?" cursed one Scout.

"Language, Ransome!" warned Mr. Fowler.

Nick fed kindling to the fire and tried to get
thirsty for the black tea brewing over the flames.
As the weather grew colder and damper, the tea
tasted better than he'd thought. In spite of the
bonfire, he was cold clear through. At last Mr.
Fowler announced, "Time to brush our teeth,
chaps. Long day tomorrow."

Boys scattered and reappeared in a line at the
stream to brush their teeth. "Up down, up down,
all around," the Scoutmaster chanted happily as
he cleaned his teeth.

Nick looked sideways at Diggery, who winked
and said, "Every trip. Likes to brush teeth, he
does."

Nick didn't warm up until he was in his sleep-

ing bag. He wormed and squirmed around, trying to shift the Welsh rocks into comfortable positions. Finally, wedged against one side of his tent, he fell asleep.

He woke up to a steady rain and realized that he was getting wet inside the sleeping bag. In the dim light, Nick scooted out of the damp sleeping bag and pulled on his warmest clothes, plus his new English boots. Wellies, they were called—short for Wellingtons. Wellies first, he slid out of his tent, to see who was awake. They couldn't camp out in a rainstorm.

And there was the stream, right at his feet. It had been many yards off when he went to sleep. Now, it thundered past the Scouts' tents, inches away.

Nick stuck his head into Diggery's tent, then Nigel's. All three of them stood and stared at the stream that had become a rushing river.

"Sod it," Diggery swore as he frowned at the stream.

"Oh, gray-ate," moaned Nigel. "Just like last time."

"It did this before when you were here?" asked Nick.

Nigel yawned and nodded. "It's a tradition.

93

Fowlsie always camps 'ere. Camped 'ere when 'ee was a Scout. Well, let's tell 'em and move the bloody tents."

In the thin, early light, everyone moved his tent to higher ground. Owl Patrol began breakfast over a fire that hissed and threatened to go out any minute, even though a pair of Owls propped a rubber groundsheet to block some of the rain.

Inside the troop tent, Nick poured a golden syrup called treacle over his porridge and dove in. He ate four slabs of bread smeared with butter and treacle, plus eggs and bacon.

"Inspection now," Diggery reminded the Pheasants. "Regulation uniform."

"In *this*?" Nick croaked, gesturing at the steady rain outside the tent.

Diggery nodded. "Just forget the rain, mate," he said. He and Nigel showed him how to display his rucksack and kit on his groundsheet outside the tent.

"Tie back your tent flaps with a slippery reef knot," Diggery said, deftly tying the ropes. "Fowler won't pass any other knot."

"I knew that," Nick said, grinning. "Just like when he was a kid, right?"

"Right," Diggery and Nigel chorused.

All the Pheasants passed inspection. Nick could see that Diggery took inspection as a personal challenge. His patrol would always know how to pass. Afterward, the troop lined up for flag raising and singing a hymn.

"Number five fifteen from *Songs of Praise*," the Scoutmaster announced.

No one had a hymnbook. All the voices began at once, singing, "He who would valiant be 'gainst all disaster, / Let him in constancy follow the Master. / There's no discouragement shall make him once relent / His first avowed intent to be a pilgrim."

Yup, Nick thought, it fits. Valiant be 'gainst all disaster. Rain dripped from his hair and face onto the uniform plastered to his body. At least he could join in on the Amen.

After the flag ceremony, they changed into trainers with no socks. "Socks only get wet," the Scoutmaster declared firmly. "Here, put these dinner packets in your rucksacks."

Mr. Fowler set a rapid pace up the first hill. Nick had thought he might get pneumonia, but maybe not at this speed.

"Twenty miles this hike," the Scoutmaster

called back over his shoulder. "We shall be the first Berkshire troop to win our hiking badge. Remember to watch for fossils, birds, animals— any odd bits to put in your reports."

Twenty miles? Nick had never hiked farther than ten. "Just twenty, huh?" he said to Diggery.

"That's what it says in the manual," Diggery replied.

"Yours is probably different from ours," said Nick.

"Don't think so, mate. Scouts started here, you know."

Nick hadn't known, but he kept quiet. If they thought English Scouts were tougher than Americans, he would show them. No matter what.

The Scouts hiked steadily, up hills and down. Nick clambered over hundreds of rocks, and always there were the sheep. He began counting them, but when he got to five hundred after only a couple miles, he quit. He looked for interesting things for his hiking report, but most of the time he had to watch his footing. Just as he was aching to sit down they stopped for dinner at Llangorse Lake.

"Here's where we'll see the Great Crested Grebe," Mr. Fowler announced. "Look sharp, now.

He lives round here."

"Who is he?" Nick asked without thinking.

Nigel bent double laughing. "Who is 'ee?" he repeated to the rest of the patrol. "Who is 'ee?" he howled again.

Embarrassed, Nick shrugged his shoulders.

"It's a bird," Diggery explained. "Naff off, Nigel. How's he supposed to know?" He turned back to Nick. "Fowler's potty over birds, right? We got our bird-watching badge last spring."

"Oh." Nick nodded toward the reeds by the lakeshore. "There's a bird. See those nice feathers on his head?"

Diggery leaned forward and grew very still. "Shh." He motioned frantically for the Scoutmaster, who inched over to the rock where Diggery, Nick, and Nigel were sitting. "There," he whispered to Mr. Fowler, and pointed to the reeds where a tan-colored bird with a green feathery crest and long, pointy bill rested in the water.

"The Great Crested Grebe!" murmured the Scoutmaster in awed tones. "Well done, Holmes. Good lad!"

"It was Nick who—" Diggery began.

Mr. Fowler shook his head. He put a finger to his mouth to signal silence and motioned the other boys to come over. All the Scouts pretended to admire the Grebe for several seconds before Mr. Fowler stood up and said, "Memorable day! The Great Crested Grebe . . . my, my. Well, now, dinner straight away. Ten miles to go before tea."

"Sir, it was Howard who spotted the Grebe, not me."

"That so, Holmes? Well," he said to Nick, "the Colonies win again." He smiled. "The one time I was in your country, Howard, I went bird-watching with my sister who lives there. I spotted an owl they'd been after for months. I'm not sure they ever forgave me."

The boys forgot the Grebe as they opened their dinner packets. Nick found a dry mixture that Diggery said was muesli, a health cereal, combined with raisins and nuts. He held up his sandwich for inspection.

"Marmite," Nigel explained. "Luv-ly."

Nick tried the marmite sandwich. It was salty, very tangy, and weird. He ate it anyway, plus the dried mixture. If I told kids at home about this, he thought, they'd never believe me. He gulped the water in his canteen. "Is this what Fowler ate on his hiking trips?" Nick asked.

Diggery nodded. "Except he says the muesli's a modern improvement."

After dinner, the rain slowed to a fine mist, and they set off again. Nick saw more sheep and more rocks plus several birds he wanted to put in his report. He found a stone with the imprint of a leaf, and later another that seemed to be the fossil of an insect.

"Hey!" Diggery said when Nick showed him the two stones. "How'd you find those?"

"Cor! Look at 'em!" Nigel exclaimed. "You're a lucky bugger! Take 'em to the British Museum. They'll know."

Other boys found rocks that appeared to have fossil remains, but none as distinct as Nick's insect one.

"You have sharp eyes, Howard," complimented Mr. Fowler. "I like that in a Scout."

Nick felt good about his eyes, but not about his feet and ankles, which hurt. But he wasn't going to complain—no way. In another hour or so, he'd have done it. Twenty long, rocky, hilly miles.

Yay! he thought. Twenty miles. In the rain. With birdseed for food. Wait till I tell the folks . . . and Marty. Nick made sure that the fossils were still in his pocket.

11

"You did what?" Mr. Howard asked as Nick dropped his tent and duffel bag in the front hall Sunday evening.

"Hiked *twenty miles*," Nick announced. "In a downpour, too, you should have seen it. And I got part of my cooking badge this morning—the way Fowler used to do it." He smiled, remembering the dreadful bread twist he had made to wind around a peeled stick and toast over the fire.

"And I found these great fossils—look!" Nick pulled the two stones from deep in his pocket. "Mom, can you take them to the British Museum to find out what they are?"

"Certainly," his mother agreed. She pointed at his uniform. "You look like you've been through a war."

"I have!" Nick started upstairs. "I want to show Marty my fossils before you take them to the museum."

Nick checked on Spike before he went into Marty's room. "Hey, little guy, how's it going?" he asked when Spike was sitting in his hand. "Did Marty feed you plenty?"

"*Errh, uunh,*" Spike grunted, his dark snout questing against Nick's shirt in hope of a treat hidden in the pocket.

Nick smiled and stroked Spike's flattened quills. "You didn't miss a thing this weekend, Spike. It rained cats and dogs and you wouldn't have liked my bread twist. It tasted gross. You ate better here at home."

Nick sat quietly on his bed for a bit, appreciating its comfort compared to the hard ground and enjoying Spike. Spike was a good listener, like Licky.

By early October, Nick had played scrum half in two more games, each time for half the game. He was getting better at passing the ball and dodging his opponents, just as Coach Stewart had promised. Classes at Baggsley-Hume were moving forward with the speed of a rugby game. Mrs. Pope said it was time for regular drama sessions to begin.

"Oh, brother!" moaned Akbar, in perfect American. It was his new and favorite phrase.

"Likewise," Nick said.

Everyone else in the class was looking expectantly at Mrs. Pope, who held an old hat in her hand. "Get in groups of five or six, please. Each group will draw an idea from the hat for its sketch. Now remember to use expression. Make it as realistic as possible."

Nick and Akbar sat very still. The rest of the kids sorted themselves into groups, first pushing all the chairs and tables to one side of the room.

"We don't need anyone to shout!" pleaded Mrs. Pope.

"Nick, Akbar! Come on, then," Diggery urged. He and Nigel, James, and Fiona were sitting on a table.

Nick and Akbar joined them on the table. Diggery went over to the hat and drew out a slip of folded paper. He plopped himself back on the table and read: "Setting: playground. Situation:

A conker fight."

"Oh, brill!" Nigel said.

"Oh, blast!" Fiona tossed her auburn hair back over her shoulders. "Who cares about conkers?"

"Everybody," James said, making a face at Fiona.

Nick said, "Everybody who knows. But *I don't.*"

"No conker fights in America?" James was appalled.

"How do I know? What do you do?"

"Conkers come from the trees," Diggery began.

"It's so bor-ring," interrupted Fiona.

Akbar gently put a hand over Fiona's mouth. "Woman must be quiet," he teased, smiling into her eyes. "These are man's things, I think."

Fiona leaned dreamily into Akbar's hand.

Mrs. Pope cleared her throat. "Is this part of your sketch?" she asked Akbar and Fiona.

Diggery, James, Nigel, and Nick snickered.

Akbar said, "Yes, Mrs. Pope. But we have not finished. Right, Fiona?" He removed his hand and sat apart.

"Right," said Fiona, eyes cast down.

"It does not look like any of the sketches I put in the hat. Get along with you now, and attend to business."

"Yes, Mrs. Pope," James said.

"Very well." She turned to face the rest of the room. "A few more minutes ought to suffice. You lot in the corner! Settle down!"

"You must explain quick these conker fights," Akbar told Diggery. "Now we are in trouble."

Diggery got off the table and stood by a window. "See the big tree by the car park? It's got conkers on it, and they're almost ready to drop."

"You wally, tell 'im they're chestnuts," Nigel said.

Diggery ignored Nigel. "You peel off the outside stuff and there's the conker! With a needle you pull a string through that's got a knot on its end."

"And soak it in vinegar to get it hard," added Nigel.

"I freeze mine," said James, "but you want to use them straight away while they're frozen."

Diggery shook his head. "Naa, it's better to bake them in the oven. Gets rid of the moisture, right? I had a ten-er last year that was baked for thirty minutes."

Nick looked blankly at Akbar.

James wailed, "It's 'opeless, they don't understand."

At home, Nick would have socked James. He'd have said, "Get on with it, scumbag!" Here, he said, "When it's got a string through it and it's hard, *what do you do with it?*"

Diggery pantomined the action. "Wrap the string around your thumb, like this, and leave a bit o' string, see? Then hit the other conker with yours. Yours is hard, right? So it smashes the other conker. Then you've got a one-er. If it smashes another conker, it's a two-er. Like that."

Mrs. Pope tapped her ruler on the desk. "Time's up!"

Akbar groaned.

"No sweat," Diggery said. "Be two teams— Nick with me and James. Akbar, you go with Nigel and Fiona. Fiona, you complain so Akbar has to put his hand over your mouth."

The first sketch was set in a department store. One girl played the part of the mother, and the rest were her kids, trying on clothes and finding fault with them, or else wanting all of them. Nick was amazed that they could be so natural in front of the class.

The next sketch took place in a car park. The driver had lost his keys and had to explain himself to his family. This group showed anger and frustration well. They sat down to much clapping.

Nick tried to melt into his chair. I can't do this, he thought. I've never done it and I can't.

"Diggery? Your group will go next," Mrs. Pope said.

The six rose to their feet. Nick and Akbar looked as if they were headed for the hangman's noose.

Diggery maneuvered Nick and James behind him. Nigel did the same with Akbar and Fiona so they appeared as two teams.

Swaggering, chin thrust out, Diggery taunted Nigel. "We've got a nineteen-er. You lot haven't a chance." He pulled an imaginary conker from his pants pocket and swung it in the air on its make-believe string.

Nick's head swiveled from side to side as he watched the imaginary conker. One student giggled and pointed at him.

"We know when we've got a winner, don't we, mate?" James elbowed Nick in the ribs.

Nick flinched as James's elbow dug in. "Uh, yeah," he said woodenly. "You guys have had it."

This time, several kids giggled. Nick froze, afraid he had used an expression that was bad in England.

Nigel swung his own imaginary conker in the air. "Take a long walk on a short pier, Duracell," he jeered.

Fiona pointed at Diggery's red hair, "Duracell! Copper-Top!" She tossed her hair back over her shoulders as if she had settled the whole affair.

Akbar stood stiffly silent.

Nigel and Diggery knelt down. Their teams followed suit. No one said anything for several seconds.

"This is much excitement," Akbar said with absolutely no expression.

At that, the giggles erupted into laughter.

Diggery went red under his freckles. "Put yours out there," he hissed at Nigel.

Nigel laid out his pretend conker with elaborate care on the schoolroom floor. No one on either team said a word. Finally Fiona squeaked, "This is so bor-ring."

Everyone in the group waited for Akbar to respond to his cue. Akbar stared at the spot where the imaginary conker lay on the floor.

Nick muttered, "Put your hand over her mouth, Akbar."

Akbar clapped a hand on Fiona's mouth so suddenly that she yelped, lurched sideways, and stepped on Nigel's hand.

"Bloody cow! Push off!" Nigel slapped Fiona's leg.

"Nigel!" Mrs. Pope said firmly. "That's un- acceptable language!"

The class hooted anyway.

Whap! Diggery brought his conker down on Nigel's.

"Smashed *yours!*" Nigel yelled before Diggery had a chance. "Now mine's a twenty! Take your team and go 'ome, joey," he said, leaping up off the floor. He made pushing motions with his hands at Diggery's group.

Diggery hung his head and gestured to Nick and James to leave the scene. They shuffled off in one direction while Nigel, Fiona, and a glassy- eyed Akbar went the other.

No one clapped. Mrs. Pope wrote something on a notepad in her lap. "I think that sketch could be improved," she said. "What would have made it stronger?"

"Ennythin'," Nicola said sourly. She was the

girl with the orange bangs and white-out fingernails.

"Didn't seem like a conker fight to *me*!"

"They didn't know what they were doing!"

"It was bor-ring!"

Fiona glared at the girl who had said it was boring. "Saw-ree," she snapped. "They don't even know what conkers are!"

Everyone looked at Nick and Akbar. Diggery said, "It's not *their* fault!"

"You're absolutely right, Diggery. I had no idea. Rotten luck you drew that particular sketch. And I reckon you haven't done this before, either of you." Mrs. Pope smiled at Nick and Akbar.

Nick tried to smile back.

Akbar said, "I am very bad. I am sorry. My father will be disappointed with me."

Mrs. Pope stood up abruptly. "Indeed he will not," she said. "You have full marks in every subject. Drama is used for enrichment, to help you lose self-consciousness when you speak. And that *will happen* as the year goes by, for both of you. Now, Nicola, Robert, let's see your effort next."

At the end of the day, Nick made a pile of

homework to take home. He had several French verbs to learn, words his classmates had known for years. He was supposed to write a poem. *Write one,* no less. He knew that his poem would be like his illustrations, his penmanship, and his acting skills. Lousy.

Beside him, Akbar was making a similar pile. He said to Nick, "In Hindi, I can write a bad poem. In English, I cannot write a poem." He shrugged his shoulders.

"I can't either." Nick started to leave the room. "Hey, why don't you come to my house?" he asked, turning to face Akbar. "My mom's crazy about stuff like poetry."

"Yes! Yes, please." Akbar snatched up his books. "My mother is waiting in the car. Your mother will tell my mother to find your house." He was smiling for the first time since they had given the disastrous sketch. "This school, it is not so easy as my father promised."

"You ain't just a-woofin'," Nick said without thinking.

"What is this *woofin'*?"

The second poetry session of the week came too soon for Nick. When Mrs. Pope announced,

"Put away maths now and get out your poems, please," he dreaded the coming hour.

"It is to die," Akbar whispered.

"Yup," Nick agreed. "Here we go. Down the tubes."

"We'll read each poem aloud," Mrs. Pope said. "We shall appreciate our poets such as Burns and Blake, or Wordsworth and Tennyson, all the more if we ourselves *write* poems. Poetry is a difficult art."

For sure, Nick thought. He and Akbar, with Mrs. Howard's encouragement, had spent a long time on their poems.

When it was Nick's turn to read his, he said, "I wrote some haiku once, in fifth grade. That's all."

"You don't need to apologize. We shall respect your poem for the time and effort you gave it," said Mrs. Pope.

The classroom was a still pond. Not a ripple on its surface. Nick thought of Akbar's words—*it is to die.*

"My poem's called 'Learning Rugby,'" he began.

"I can't 'ear 'im," James sang out.

"'Learning Rugby,' you wally," Nick said.

Somehow, that helped. " 'Learning Rugby,' " he said for the third time, his voice stronger.

> "I think that I shall never see
> A game as tough as ol' rugby,
> A game that slams you in the mud
> And leaves you feeling like a dud.
> A game that pounds you in the scrum.
> You stop to rub your poor, sore bum.
> The coach says, 'Lads, we need a try,'
> The players don't ask how or why.
> They score the try."

For a second, the stillness held. Then Diggery said, "Smashing!"

James's whistle split the air.

"Cor!" sighed Nicola.

Mrs. Pope began to clap. The whole room clapped. "Excellent, Nicholas," Mrs. Pope said when her voice could be heard. "We'll have no more apologies from you!"

Nick was solid red—a human beet. But a happy beet.

Mrs. Pope stood up. "Your poem was good because it gave us the feel of rugby in a few words.

You used some British slang, as well. That's very interesting. Do you mind if I ask what you Americans say for 'bum'?" She stopped, embarrassed. "Now, this talk is a secret, class. Your parents might not understand."

Akbar leaned toward Nick. "My father . . ." he said, shaking his head.

Mrs. Pope waited for Nick to speak.

"Uh, well, we say rear, or bottom, or butt, I guess." Nick felt as if he had turned red permanently.

"In French," Mrs. Pope said, "we would say *derrière*. That's my favorite. It is rather elegant, don't you think?"

"*Derrière*," the class repeated. Finally, a useful French word.

Two more students read their poems, and then it was Akbar's turn. "I wish my funeral pyre to be in India," he whispered to Nick as he stood up.

"Yours is better than mine," Nick said encouragingly.

Akbar stood tall. "This is about the Raj. That is Hindi for the *reign* or the *rule*." He glanced around the room uncertainly.

The teacher said, "Yes. You are referring to

the period when Britain ruled over India. She no longer does, of course. The Empire is over."

"The title is 'After the Raj,' " said Akbar.

> "My father tells me they were here,
>   the English.
> I did not see them, I was unborn.
> They were the Raj.

> "They are gone now,
>   the English.
> Still India remains.
> India in pieces, my father says,
>   after the Raj.

> "Now she must work, my country,
>   after the Raj."

No one moved. Akbar stared down at his poem, then began to fold the paper, over and over, into tiny squares.

Mrs. Pope found her voice. "Please, Akbar, don't fold it. It belongs on the headmaster's bulletin board."

Yay! Nick thought.

Mrs. Pope took the poem and smoothed it out

on the table. "It is very moving," she said quietly. "You know only a few English words, but you use them with great effect. Someday, we want you to tell us about India."

She turned to the class. "I would also like your poem, Nicholas, and Nigel's and Alison's. The headmaster will wish to display them. This class is going to teach the rest of the school something about poetry this term!"

Akbar sat down. He was trying not to look proud. "We shall not have the funeral yet," he told Nick.

Nick beamed back at him. They had survived another of England's tests, this time with full marks.

12

The following Sunday at noon, the Howards prepared to go to an At Home party on their street. Nick polished one shoe on the back of his trouser leg and thought of the five new conkers he had baked to rock hardness, or so he hoped. Conker fights were the way to spend October Sundays.

"I wanta stay home," Gus said mutinously.

"No way, José," said Mr. Howard as he stood behind Gus to fix his tie. "This is our official welcome to the neighborhood, and we're all expected to show up."

Marty sighed noisily. "I could be at school, playing Frisbee with the boarders. It's a blast there on weekends."

"I don't know why they want kids at the party," Nick said. "And I can't get the mud out of my fingernails."

"When you tell them how we beat the socks off Windsor-Eton this morning," his dad said, "they won't care about the mud."

"Hugh, really!" said Mrs. Howard.

Four houses down Kings' Ride, Mr. Howard knocked on the door of their hosts, Colonel and Mrs. Haltwhistle.

"Remember that we are America's ambassadors," Mr. Howard whispered. "Best manners, everyone."

Colonel Haltwhistle opened the door just as Gus said, "I wanta go home!"

Erect, white-haired, and spectacled, the colonel bent stiffly forward. "You may not go home, young man, until you pet my pussycat."

Nick and Marty were glad to see that Gus looked very embarrassed. He recovered quickly. "Hi," Gus said, sticking out his right hand.

"How d'ye do," Colonel Haltwhistle said, shaking hands. "You must play with our cat, you see, because our grandchildren are not here often enough."

He straightened up. "Do come in and meet your neighbors. Everyone is eager to know the Americans on Kings' Ride."

Mrs. Haltwhistle, a tiny woman in a flowered dress, was careful to see that the Howards met everyone at the party. Nick and Marty stood to one side of the drawing room and drank lemonade. Nick was wondering how long they'd have to stay when Colonel Haltwhistle joined them.

"I hear you're scrum half for Baggsley this season, Nicholas. I was scrum half, as well, sixty-some years ago."

"Whooee," Nick said.

"Yes . . . whooee," the colonel echoed, lingering over the word. Laugh lines creased his elderly face. "You Americans have certainly changed the language. And our lives," he added thoughtfully. "I remember praying for you to come over during the war. Our boys couldn't go it alone."

"Were you in the army then, sir?" Marty asked.

"My, yes. We all were, actually. Heavy rationing, don't you know. Mrs. Haltwhistle and the children had one egg apiece for an entire month. A few ounces of washing powder for the laundry. No chocolates or roasts or anything good like that. No sugar. No petrol to speak of." He cleared his throat. "Did you know about that?"

Nick and Marty shook their heads. "Could you

tell us some more?" Nick asked. "That's the only kind of history I like. War is interesting."

"Only if you've never been in one." The colonel put a veined hand on Nick's shoulder. "You come back sometime when we don't have guests, and I'll tell you about wars. Then, perhaps, you won't feel the need to be part of one."

The colonel patted Nick's shoulder warmly, then Marty's, before he moved to another group of guests.

"Can you hear that lady in the black dress talking about the hedgehogs in her garden?" Marty whispered.

Nick whispered back, "We ought to try another hedgehog party tonight. They know each other better now. Maybe they won't fight over the food this time."

Promptly at two o'clock, as though a bell had rung, everyone said, "Oh, we must be leaving." When the others were all gone, each of the Howards thanked the Haltwhistles for the party.

On the way home, Mr. Howard suddenly clapped Marty and Nick on the shoulders. "You know, guys, it's been so long since I had an American hamburger, I'm growing weak. Let's go to that McDonald's in Windsor."

"Can I take off these dumb clothes first?" Gus asked.

"Sundays in Windsor are pretty crowded, I hear," said Mrs. Howard. "All those dreadful American tourists."

Mr. Howard chuckled. "They sure mess up the country, don't they? What the heck, let's go anyway."

It was only a ten-minute trip into Windsor by car, and they were soon walking through the doorway of McDonald's.

"Surprise!" hollered Diggery.

James let go with his earsplitting whistle.

"A most happy un-birthday, Nicholas," Akbar said.

Nigel and two other boys from Nick's class yelled, "Happy un-birthday! happy un-birthday!"

"Well, holy crud," Marty said to Nick.

His dad asked, "Were you surprised, Nick?"

"Well, yeah! My birthday's in July!"

Mrs. Howard was all smiles. "I remember, and it was a horrible day. Sticky hot, and poor little Gooney Pig died, and we were getting everything ready for the movers. We thought you deserved a real birthday."

She reached into her purse. "Here. You pay for what your friends want, and sit together. We'll sit at another table. Afterward we're going back to the house for cake and a movie and a darts tournament. Okay?"

It was more than okay. As he got into bed that night, Nick knew it had been a great un-birthday. And in the garage was a new BMX bicycle. He could have races with Diggery or Nigel . . . or anyone else who wanted to.

His dad had said, "Now I can use your ten-speed to go for rides with Mom. Pretty clever of me, huh?"

Oh yes, Nick thought, very clever. The BMX was given to him in England. It was a reason for him to like living here.

He heard the train chuff into the Baggsley station and out again. He'd be on that train with Nigel and Diggery on Wednesday, going to Virginia Water, where there were BMX trails around the lake. Here, you could take your bike on the train.

Nick flopped uncomfortably in bed. He hated it when his mind went around in circles this way.

"Hey, Nick?" Marty and Gus came in the door.

"What did you get for the hedgehog party?"

Nick sat up. "Geez, I forgot."

Marty set Pokey on the floor. Pokey stayed curled into a prickly ball. "I'll find something in the fridge. Get Spike out so Pokey calms down. He squeaked and squeaked at me when I picked him up."

"Mrs. Tiggy-Winkle, too," Gus said, trying to soothe his smaller hedgehog. "Maybe she's tired."

Nick dug a protesting Spike out of his nest as Marty tiptoed downstairs to the kitchen. The three hedgehogs grunted and woofled at one another briefly, then were silent. Spike raised his black snout in the air, tested Nick's finger with his pink tongue, then hunkered on the floor.

"You're doing what?" Mrs. Howard's voice carried from the downstairs to the second floor.

"Uh-oh," Nick said. "Get in my closet, Gus, and be real quiet! Mom must've caught Marty in the kitchen." He shoved his brother into the closet and dumped all the hedgehogs on his lap. "Remember, not a sound!"

"Eeee! Eeee!" Mrs. Tiggy-Winkle cried, frightened by the quick movements.

Nick dove back into bed. One hedgehog—he wasn't sure which—kept up a steady, shrill complaint. If his mom came into the room, it was all over.

"They're pokin' me!" Gus hissed from inside the closet.

"Shut up!" Nick hissed back.

Finally, Marty slid through the door and shut it soundlessly behind him. "Be real quiet," he warned. "Mom's still up and she's suspicious."

Nick let Gus and the hedgehogs out of the closet while Marty set out their food. He had brought a glass of milk that Nick poured into Spike's dish, an aluminum pie pan.

"I had to make this sandwich because Mom stood right there," Marty said, crumbling bread and bits of ham into the milk. "She knows something's up because I ate all that cake and ice cream and she says I can't possibly be hungry."

Spike's snout quivered as he smelled the ham. When Nick set him near the pie pan, Spike waded into the center of it and began gulping noisily.

Pokey moved toward the pan, grunted once, and put his front feet into the milk. He tasted it, but did not seem hungry. Mrs. Tiggy-Winkle sorted fussily through the bits of bread and ham. When Spike got too close, she snarled at him.

"I think they want to hibernate," Marty said.

"I read about them in a book at school. They're not real whipped up about people—and they hibernate *all winter*. We ought to put them back in the garden."

"Geez, not yet, Marty. I . . . I really like having him in my closet," Nick said. He wasn't going to tell about the private talks he had with Spike. Marty'd think he was a baby, pouring out his thoughts to an animal. "Just a bit longer, okay? Then we'll make holes for them in that haystack behind the hedge."

Gus scratched one leg. "They've got fleas, you know," he grumbled. "And now they're on *me!*"

Spike burped wetly and waddled out of the pie pan. Mrs. Tiggy-Winkle sneezed milk onto Pokey, who shook himself and growled at her to get out of the way. *"Eee,"* she whimpered before burping louder than Spike.

Nick grinned. Who'd have thought they'd have so much personality? He watched Spike amble off to inspect his sneakers. Spike didn't seem as sluggish as the other two. Maybe he was younger, Nick thought.

When neither Pokey nor Mrs. Tiggy-Winkle moved around the room, Marty got bored. "I'm going to bed," he said, picking up Pokey. "Come on, Gus, it's late."

Nick put Spike back into his newspaper nest, hid the empty pie pan, and got back into bed. He didn't want to think about returning Spike to the garden. It'd be different if Licky were here, he thought—if I just had Licky.

Every week when Nick visited his cat, he told him he'd be coming home in February. *February.* Nick sighed. He heard the train pull in again, but he had fallen asleep before it drew away from the station.

13

By November Nick appreciated his sweater, even if it was purple. Mrs. Pope kept opening windows for fresh air.

"I feel like a grape ice lolly," Nick grumbled to Akbar one afternoon.

"I wear the winter underwear from Marks and Spencer's," Akbar whispered back. "Soon now, we can go home to sit on our radiators."

Mrs. Pope tapped her ruler on the desk. "Before school is out, remember that we have a history test on Friday before we go to the Victoria and Albert Museum. Nicholas and Akbar, I have special work sheets for you. You may not know all of the monarchs in order as we do."

Alarm bells clanged in Nick's mind. Monarchs in order? All of them? There was no way.

"And remember Guy Fawkes Night, tomorrow evening at seven-thirty, for you and all of your families."

The buzzer sounded, and the second they were dismissed, students bolted for the door. Nick and Akbar went up to Mrs. Pope's desk for their work sheets. "No one needs to know all the kings and queens in order," Nick said, amazed at his bravery. It was the first time he had told her what he thought of British education.

"Codswallop. You Americans learn your presidents. Simply sing these names in order, as they appear, to the tune of 'Good King Wenceslas.' You'll know them by midweek."

Nick and Akbar took the work sheets and headed for the outdoors. "Willie, Willie, Harry, Ste / Harry, Dick, John, Harry Three," Nick sang slowly, fitting the names to the tune. "Well, *maybe*," he said to Akbar.

"Is this a Christian song?"

"Mm-hm, it's a Christmas carol. Aw, rats!" Nick said, when it hit him. Akbar would not have celebrated Christmas in Delhi, India.

"Yes, rats," Akbar repeated solemnly. "You

will teach me the song?"

"Sure. Tomorrow afternoon. Ask your mom, okay?"

Akbar left in the car with his mother. While Nick waited for Mrs. Howard, he tried to repeat the first two lines he had sung to Akbar. "Willie, Willie, Harry—"

Nigel was hopping from one foot to the other, looking bored, as he waited to be picked up. "Did you know *nick* means steal?" he asked, interrupting the song.

Nick tried to hold on to his temper. "It doesn't mean that in America—only *here!*" he retorted. Not for the first time, he wondered if Nigel was jealous. He knew that Nigel thought of Diggery as his best friend. So he wouldn't punch him out—not yet anyway.

"Aaa, come off it, Nigel." Diggery left the group he'd been with and came to stand by Nick. "Nigel can't keep his gob shut," Diggery said with a wicked grin. He swerved as Nigel aimed a blow at his chest.

"When're we going to Virginia Water again?" Diggery asked, dancing away from Nigel. "Those trails are smashing."

"Right!" Nigel agreed, landing a friendly blow

on Diggery's arm.

"Anytime," Nick said hastily. He wasn't comfortable enough to fight with anyone yet, not even a mock fight like this one. "We should ask Akbar. His BMX is really cool."

Nigel's face darkened. " 'After the Raj'? Huh! That Paki thinks 'ee's too good for us, 'ee does."

"Oh, get stuffed! He's from India." Diggery gave Nigel a friendly jab in the stomach.

Nigel's mother arrived then, and he left, calling back, "How about tomorrow?"

"How about tomorrow?" Diggery repeated to Nick.

"I can't," Nick said, remembering his promise to Akbar. "What's a Paki?"

"A Pakistani," replied Diggery. "My mum and dad think they should stay in their own country."

Nick tried to remember the globe in their family room. "Wasn't Pakistan made out of India? I mean, didn't it used to be one country?"

"I think so, mate. But *we're* not very big. Mum and Dad say we don't have room for that lot, or jobs, right?" Diggery moved toward the bike rack. "I have to go home."

He got on his bike and swung around by Nick.

"About Akbar," he said, pedaling slowly. "He's fine by me, but there's Nigel, you know?"

When Nick got into the car with his mother, he told her what Nigel and Diggery had just said. "Akbar's plenty nice," Nick said. "The girls all like him. Those guys don't because he's from India."

"I think," she said after a bit, "that Britain didn't realize how many of her colonists would want to come here someday. Once England was an empire, but now it's a pretty small island. And right now there's a shortage of jobs."

"Do they hate us, too?"

"As a country, yes, some of them do. We're different. We're large and wealthy and we throw our weight around. If you think of England as the parent and us as her child . . . well, we're a big, bossy child at times."

"But Colonel Haltwhistle said he prayed for us to come!"

"True, and we wanted to help in the war, Nick. But people desperate for help—people dependent on others—dislike having to be grateful afterward. Everyone wants to be independent, to go it alone. Everyone wants that."

Nick leaned back against the car seat and

closed his eyes. They love me and they hate me. I didn't want to come here, and they didn't want me to. Great.

"We have our own racial problems and discrimination in America, too, Nick. We just don't see it in our hometown. As for Akbar, he's a terrific person. Diggery and Nigel will see that in time."

"Is our whole family going to Guy Fawkes Night?" Nick asked, wanting to change the subject.

"Yes, I'm making a dessert for it. But you have to tell us about Guy Fawkes. You're the only one getting good British history. My study course doesn't start till after New Year's."

Good British history? There was no such thing. "I hate history," he shouted.

"Nicholas Howard! You'll make me have an accident!"

That night at dinner, Mrs. Howard said, "We will now have a lecture from the resident history professor. Ta da!"

"Willie, Willie, Harry, Ste—" Nick sang.

"What's that?" asked his father.

"The British kings and queens. In order."

Mrs. Howard said, "First, tell us about Guy Fawkes."

Gus began to slide off his chair.

"No you don't, bud. Listen up," Mr. Howard said to Gus.

Nick took a deep breath. "Guy Fawkes was part of something called the Gunpowder Plot. It was November fourth, just like today, only back in 1605."

"My brother, the Ohio Brain," Marty said.

"He tunneled into a basement under the House of Lords," Nick went on, "and stuffed it full of gunpowder. It was supposed to blow everybody up on November fifth—the king, Parliament, everybody. Only they found him out, and nothing blew up, and he and his helpers were executed. So now we have Guy Fawkes Day."

"He was a bad guy—pardon the pun," Marty said with a grin, "so why are we having a party?" He peered over the top of his glasses at Nick.

"Because it didn't blow up, nerd."

"At least the House of Lords had a basement," Mrs. Howard said. "I wish we had one."

"Can I go now?" Gus asked.

"You help Marty and Nick clean up the kitchen," said his mother. "Dad and I are going to watch the news on TV."

When their parents had left the kitchen, Marty asked Nick, "Can you really say all the kings and queens in order?"

"Maybe. There's a special way to do it, see?"

Marty read Nick's work sheet while Nick sang to the tune of "Good King Wenceslas."

"Willie, Willie, Harry, Ste,
Harry, Dick, John, Harry Three.
One, Two, Three Neds, Richard Two,
Henry Four, Five, Six, then Who?
Edward Four, Five, Dick the Bad,
Harrys Twain and Ned the Lad.
Mary, Bessie, James the Vain,
Charlie, Charlie, James again.
William and Mary, Anna Gloria,
Four Georges, William, and Victoria—"

Nick stopped short. "That's all I know. There're a few more, though, and the queen we've got now, Bessie Two."

Marty looked up from the paper. "I have to have this. Freshmen do world history here. So we both got lucky. Ha!"

"I just knew this country would be stuffed

with it," Nick said as he carried plates to the sink.

"I need food for Mrs. Tiggy-Winkle," Gus announced.

"Oh yeah. Hey, Gus, how's your closet?"

Gus shrugged. "Okay. She just sleeps now, like Marty said. How many days till we get our cats back? Fishhead plays with me *whenever I want*."

The next night was mild, with a star-filled sky. All the Baggsley-Hume students, plus parents and kids from Boadicea First School, were on hand for the huge bonfire celebrating the failure of Guy Fawkes.

"Akbar's here!" Nick said, "Come on, Marty."

As the crowd became noisier, Nick, Marty, and Akbar were drawn to the site of the bonfire. The headmaster lit the fire, above which hung an effigy of Guy Fawkes. One foot, then two, glowed red-orange in the night. Flames licked the dummy's trousers and raced upward to its chest.

Nick shuddered. It would be terrible to be burned alive.

Diggery, James, and Nigel dashed into view. "Yo, Diggery!" Nick hollered, waving at them to come over.

The games master and headmaster began shooting off fireworks. Splashes of red exploded in the sky. An electric blue burst against the darkness and sifted colorfully downward. Glorious Catharine wheels followed Roman candles, with rip-raps giving off their satisfactory, loud bangs. Golden stars and white stars mingled way overhead. It did not last long enough. Fireworks always ended before people were tired of seeing them, Nick thought.

The effigy burned down to its stick. Guy Fawkes had lost again. Nick, Marty, Akbar, Diggery, James, and Nigel trooped into the gym to enjoy the refreshments that always accompanied Guy Fawkes Night.

"It was good of Mr. Fawkes to get caught," Akbar observed, his mouth full of Mrs. Howard's brownies. "Shall we have the American hot dog as well?"

"They're for summer cookouts," Nick said. "And baseball. You can't watch baseball without hot dogs."

"I know baseball!" Akbar said. "American businessman, a friend of my father's, lived with us during two years. He taught me baseball. I can hit the home run."

"Brill! You and Nick can teach us!" Diggery reached for another brownie.

"Baseball's in spring," Nick said uneasily, picturing himself in the spring, at home, on the diamond behind his own school.

"We've got American football now," James reminded them. "We 'aven't learned it yet. Nick keeps changin' the rules, 'ee does." He grinned at Nigel and Diggery.

"I don't either!" protested Nick. "We just get them mixed up with rugby. Somebody always forgets."

"You guys ever do any schoolwork?" Marty teased.

"Not if we can help it, mate," replied Diggery.

"Oh, brother," Akbar said. "I must know to sing 'Willie, Willie' by Friday."

That night, as Nick got into bed, he told himself he would write Bobby—that turkey. Even if he hadn't written, Nick missed him. They'd been friends since nursery school. With Bobby he could say anything and be understood. It was a big maybe, but maybe his parents would let him *phone* Bobby. Now there was a smashing idea.

137

14

Nick made a strong case for his phone call to Bobby. As Thanksgiving neared, Nick was still lobbying for the call.

"Oh, all right," his mother said the week of Thanksgiving. "It's only natural to be thinking of home now. I know *I* am."

"Thanks, Mom! I won't talk a real long time, promise." Nick could tell from his mother's face that she wasn't thinking of home or Bobby, but of her own son.

"Jut will be here soon, Mom, only a couple weeks. And we'll have Marty's boarders for the big dinner . . . and Akbar and Diggery. They're real excited about coming to an American Thanksgiving."

His mother gave him a swift hug. "You're becoming a very perceptive person, you know that? You can call tomorrow noon when you get home for half day. It'll be morning in the States then, before Bobby goes to school."

Nick dialed the many-digit international call himself. He gripped the phone receiver tightly as he heard Bobby's phone ring over three thousand miles away.

"Wexlers, Bobby speaking."

"Hey! It's me, Nick."

"Nick who?"

"Nick Howard, gerbil-brain! Who else?"

"Really? You callin' from way over in England?"

"Of course I am! How's it going over there?"

"Okay, I guess. Great high school football, but *our* team's lousy. Nobody likes the coach much."

Nick's own coach came clearly to mind. "My rugby coach is super. Yells his head off, but he really knows the game."

"Oh, yeah? What's it like?"

"Like football, only rougher. And faster. No pads . . . and we get hit a lot—especially me, because I play scrum half." He waited for Bobby to be impressed.

"Oh yeah? What's that?"

"A great position!" he said, frustrated, knowing he could never make it clear on the phone. "Look, how's Tom and Jason? It wouldn't kill anybody to write. Especially Sally. She said she would."

Bobby laughed. "*She* might, but, you know, guys don't write letters. Writing is dumb. What would I write about?"

"Everything!" Nick could imagine what would happen if he told Mrs. Pope that writing was dumb. She'd probably bop him on the head with her ruler. "We write papers all the time here," he said. "We even write poetry. In real ink. And with illustrations."

"How can you stand it?" Now Bobby was impressed.

"Well, it's tough. I mean, really tough. I'm the worst in the class." Not in poetry, of course, but no way would Bobby understand that.

Bobby laughed again. "Worst in the class? Wait'll I tell the guys!"

"Geez, thanks a lot! I'm not failing or anything! What's the matter with you?"

Costly international seconds ticked away. Finally, Bobby asked, "What're you doing over there, anyway?"

Nick told himself that this was Bobby Wexler, friend of a lifetime. He just can't know what it's like here, Nick thought, and that's the problem.

"I'm in Scouts now," Nick said, hoping to have hit on a safe subject. "We've been hiking in Wales already. *Twenty miles in the rain!* And I brought back real fossils. One's some kind of insect. You should see it!"

"You went to Wales? Wow! Where's that?"

"Just next door. Only a few hours away. We went on a bus and camped in the mountains. Well, low mountains. My whole weekend only cost ten pounds."

"How much?"

"About fifteen dollars. A pound's about a dollar and a half in America. *We* couldn't go *anywhere* for a whole weekend that cheap, see what I mean?"

"Uh-huh. You been to visit the Queen yet? My mom said you lived next to Windsor Castle."

"Nobody visits the Queen, you dork. Mom's been on castle tours, though. Maybe Marty and I'll go, now that most of the dumb tourists have gone home."

"Dumb tourists, huh?"

Nick remembered what it had been like to

elbow their way through Windsor in late August and September. Remembered the shopkeepers' remarks after a busload of tourists had stormed through. "Well, they aren't very polite," he told Bobby. "They gripe about everything, at least some of them do."

Bobby was silent.

Nick said, "Tell me about everybody. What's happening? Did you get Mr. Steckler for a teacher like you wanted?"

Bobby talked then. Every few words he said "like" or "you know," which sounded funny on the phone. It would be better in person, Nick thought. Static crackled on the line, so that Nick missed words here and there.

"Everything's about the same, you know," Bobby said. "I saw Jut at Homecoming, with Gwen. She was a queen's attendant, you know. Long dresses . . . and the guys wore suits. They looked, like, different."

"Mm-hmm." Nick thought of the things he had wanted Bobby to know. About conker fights and BMX trails in Windsor Park and Virginia Water. Diggery and Akbar, even Nigel. How you could take your bike on the train. Watching out for the IRA bombs. Having to recite every single British king and queen, and in perfect order. But he knew now that Bobby couldn't understand. He didn't even sound very interested.

"I promised Mom I wouldn't talk too long, okay? You say *hi* to Tom and Jason. And Sally. Her arm wouldn't drop off if she wrote. Tell her I said that."

"Okay. Thanks for calling, Nick. You should call again sometime. This was cool. 'Bye." Bobby hung up.

Nick put the receiver down. So. Bobby wanted *him* to call back. "HA!" Nick said to the empty kitchen.

Gus charged in, papers dropping from his arms like giant confetti. "Where's Mom? I've got all my stories. Mrs. Cameron let us bring 'em home. Mine're the best. You wanta play marbles? I just learned a really cool shot."

"Relaxez-vous, Gus! Mom's upstairs, and I don't want to play marbles. Just get lost."

"Well, ex-kew-ooz ME!" Gus hollered as Nick stomped upstairs. Nick slammed his door and got out *Winnie-the-Pooh*. He didn't want to think about anything else right now.

Thanksgiving Day was special only to the Americans in England. Nick and his brothers went to school as if it were any Thursday, and

Mr. Howard went to work.

This first Thanksgiving away from home, Mrs. Howard was cooking every traditional food she could manage to find in the specialty shops. Their British oven would barely hold the huge turkey, so she borrowed a neighbor's roaster oven to bake the sweet-potato casserole, rolls, and extra stuffing. Pecan and pumpkin pies sat on the counter under linen cloths.

Nick brought Diggery and Akbar straight to the kitchen when they got home from school on Thursday. "Aah," Akbar breathed when Nick lifted the cloth on a pie.

"When do we eat?" Diggery asked, peering into the oven at the turkey. "Cor! It's ginormous!"

"Thank you, thank you," replied Mrs. Howard as she dashed into the kitchen. She was all dressed up. "I forgot to baste him at three!"

Nick took Akbar and Diggery up to his room to hear the new tape Jut had sent. They crunched apples and laughed at Bill Cosby, who was as popular in England as he was in America, but mainly they thought about the dinner.

At six o'clock, the school bus arrived with Marty and his boarder friends just as Mr. Howard drove in the driveway. Everyone gathered in the front hall for introductions.

"This is Rajeev," Marty said, "from Delhi."

Rajeev inclined his head toward Mr. and Mrs. Howard, then Akbar. "Rajeev Ashim Subooha. I am delighted to be here," he said, with only a trace of accent. "I've lived in four countries now, but I've never had an American Thanksgiving. And I eat like a horse." He patted his stomach.

"Your English . . ." Mr. Howard began.

"Is magnificent. I know. I am only a fake Indian. All this washes off." He rubbed his cheeks.

Akbar, beaming, edged over toward Rajeev.

A deep, rich voice broke in, "Enough, man. It's my turn." The voice belonged to the tallest of the boys, who held out his hand to Mrs. Howard, then Mr. Howard.

"I'm Mufu Thapelo Fashina, from Nigeria. And if *he*"—with a nod at Rajeev—"eats like a horse, then *I* eat like an elephant." His smile was dazzling as he shook hands.

Gus hurtled down the steps just as Mufu was looking for another hand to shake. "Hey, short stuff, I'm Mufu," he said to Gus.

"Who-fu?" Gus asked, looking up into the shining black face with its wonderful smile. "You oughta do teeth commercials."

"GUS!" said four horrified family members at once.

Mufu roared with laughter and swung Gus up onto his shoulders. "You can't get down till you can say Mufu Thapelo Fashina, you hear?"

Marty whispered to Nick. "Aren't they cool? There's nobody in my class like this back home."

Nick nodded, overcome. By then, Rajeev was talking with Akbar and Mufu had convulsed Diggery with some remark. The noise level in the hall would cover anything but a bullhorn, Nick decided. "Are they older?" he asked in a normal tone.

"Yeah, about sixteen. They've lived all over. That's why they're still freshmen. I think Rajeev speaks four languages . . . and Mufu speaks at least three." Marty shrugged. "Shows you how much *we* know, hunh?"

Mrs. Howard shooed everyone into the dining room so that dinner could begin. Nick lit the candles in the center of the table and showed Diggery and Akbar where to sit.

"I think we'll let the littlest ask the blessing," Mr. Howard said.

Gus bowed his head and prayed, "Rub-a-dub-

dub, Thanks for the grub, Ya-ay, Jesus!"

"GUS!" his family exclaimed again.

Mr. Howard's voice overrode the hilarity. "Young man!"

Gus shrank down in his seat and grew very quiet.

Mr. Howard bowed his head, "Lord, thank You for this special Thanksgiving and for the new friends who are with us tonight. Help us to be grateful for every day on earth and everything we have been given. Thank you for America, our country, and for India, home of Akbar and Rajeev. For Nigeria, which gave us Mufu, and for England, Diggery's home before it was ours. Help us to grow in love and understanding of one another. Amen."

He stood up then. "The ritual carving ceremony will now begin. Watch closely as the clumsy father butchers yet another turkey."

"He's not kidding," Nick told Akbar and Diggery. "Jut's the only one in the family who does it right."

"I'm so sorry Jut isn't here," Mrs. Howard said. "He would love to meet all of you."

"Oh, we can come back, can't we, Mufu?" Rajeev said.

"Sure can." Mufu's smile broadened as his plate was heaped with turkey.

"You boys talk just like Americans," Mrs. Howard said.

"Isn't it terrible?" Mufu said solemnly. "The American kids at our school are such a bad influence. Me mum is 'opin' I'll speak proper English, she is, but it's 'opeless!"

Diggery choked with laughter and mashed potatoes. Akbar pounded him on the back till he could breathe again.

"Perhaps I will be at your school next year," Akbar told Rajeev. "It is called the seventh grade. If my parents move, I must be a boarder, like you."

"We have a ball. I can swear in twenty-six languages." Rajeev winked at Akbar, then Diggery. "You guys come to school with Nick and Marty some weekend and we'll teach you. We think Marty has a natural talent for languages."

Nick, Diggery and Akbar grinned at one another as Marty blushed.

"Mm-mmm," Diggery sighed, swallowing a bite of sweet-potato casserole. "If I were an American, I'd eat this meal every Sunday, I would. Can my mum get these foods?"

Mrs. Howard laughed. "Yes, if she's willing

to go to London and Ascot to the delicatessens. I had quite a time—especially finding the tinned pumpkin—but I was a determined woman. We always have the same things at Thanksgiving."

"Excuse, please. Why is that?" Akbar asked.

"Tradition," Nick explained. "We're big on tradition."

Akbar still looked confused. "Everyone in America?"

"Yup," Nick said, happily forking in turkey buried in gravy. "The Pilgrims ate this same stuff with the Indians at the first harvest, after they'd had a really bad winter. Lots died, see? And these were their first crops. They ate turkey, because that's what lived around there. I guess it was the first time they knew they were going to make it in America. So it was a big deal."

Diggery and Akbar looked at one another, as if the mystery were finally cleared up.

"Thanks, mate. Good story," Diggery said. "You lot have smashing holidays. I've seen Halloween in movies—and some schools lay on a bit of something—but not like in America."

"Guy Fawkes Night was great," Nick said politely, refusing to think about the pillowcase full of candy he would have collected at home on Halloween.

"Holidays, pooey," Mrs. Howard said. "I love what there is to see and do here that we don't have at home. The beautiful manor houses, and the castles . . ."

"Sight-seeing . . . aargh," said Rajeev, with an understanding smile for Mrs. Howard. "My parents live in north England and they are always asking what museum I have been to—what famous building? Maybe when I am older. Now, when they ask me to go with them I say, 'ABC?' "

"ABC?" echoed Mrs. Howard.

"Another Bloody Castle," Rajeev and Mufu said together.

Diggery giggled. "That's a good one, that is. My mum and dad are always—"

"And *mine*," Akbar interrupted. "All those famous, dark little paintings." He shook his head sadly.

"But that's one reason we came," said Mrs. Howard. "To see famous things and go to places we've always heard about."

"Do not misunderstand, Mrs. Howard," Mufu said, sounding suddenly adult. "We see these things on school trips, and we remember them, but this"—he gestured around the table—"this is why we are here." Again, the smile.

Nick looked gratefully at Mufu. "Can Akbar and Diggery and I really come to school with Marty and see you guys?"

"Sure!" Mufu said. "Lots of empty beds on weekends, man. Come some Saturday on the train and just stay over."

Diggery and Akbar nodded happily at Nick.

"Could we have our pie now?" Gus asked softly.

When Rajeev looked at his watch and said they must be going, everyone protested. "We can come back anytime," he said. "This is the best food, with the nicest people, in all England. But if we're not in for bed check . . . the ax will fall." He made chopping motions on his neck.

Mr. Howard and Marty walked Mufu and Rajeev to the train station. Nick and his mom drove Diggery and Akbar home.

"Thanksgiving is luv-ly," Diggery said. "My mum will ring you about the recipes, Mrs. Howard."

"My mother also. We must learn to know the Subooha family. Rajeev is *cool*," said Akbar.

"Just listen to him, " Mrs. Howard said. "We're already messing up his perfect English."

15

After the talk over Thanksgiving dinner, Nick's mom became very stubborn about sight-seeing. "It would be just stupid to live here and not see these things," she told Nick and Marty. "And that's the end of it."

On Saturday, the family piled into the car and drove to Windsor, headed for the castle in the center of town.

"Hugh! You're driving just the way they do!"

"Now, Rae, he was pooping along at fifty and so I passed him. I thought you were going to tell us about the castle."

"If I live long enough," Mrs. Howard said.

Marty whispered to Nick, "Another fun-filled family outing."

The Howards entered the castle grounds by

way of the King Henry VIII gate. "See those holes over the gateway?" Mrs. Howard pointed overhead. "If we were enemies, they'd pour boiling oil through those holes to keep us out."

"If somebody did it now, we could go home," Nick said.

"But if we were friends," continued Mrs. Howard, "we might be bringing a snack with us— maybe stuffed dormouse in a little clay dish. They had take-out dormouse shops just like we have hamburger places today."

"Is a dormouse like a hedgehog?" Gus asked, alarmed.

Marty spoke fast. "Not at all, no way." He looked around inside the castle walls. "Hey, Gus, look at those uniforms! How about those hats?"

They watched a Coldstream guard in a tall, black, furry hat stomp his feet, shoulder his rifle, and pace away from his tiny guard's house. A nearby guard did the same. They each whirled, stomped again, and paced back to their houses. After more foot stomping, they stood at attention in the doorways, rifles resting on the ground.

"You can see why they need those thick-soled shoes," Mr. Howard observed.

"Can you eat hedgehogs, too?" Gus shrilled.

Nick grabbed Gus's hand. "Come on, let's look at the moat," he said, pulling Gus behind him.

For the rest of their tour through the castle and St. George's Chapel, Nick and Marty worried that Gus would keep mentioning hedgehogs. Gus was incredibly persistent.

But Gus wandered away from the family, and by the time a guard returned him, no one was thinking about hedgehogs.

"Now we'll catch up with your mother," Mr. Howard said, as he gripped Gus's hand. "She should be on the queen's side of the castle by now." He chuckled. "She'd love a house designed this way—one whole side to herself. I wonder where they kept the kids?"

"With their nannies, where they belonged," Nick said, frowning down at Gus.

"You 'n' Marty think you're so smart. P. I. J.!" Gus made a face at Nick.

"What's a P. I. J.?" asked Mr. Howard.

"Poop in a jar," Nick answered. "That's what he calls us when he's really ticked off."

"I see," said their father.

Nick knew how Gus felt. Marty had too often made him feel the same way. Not lately, of course. Lately everything had been different. Different for Gus, too, he thought.

"You can't run away like that, Gus," Nick said more gently. "It scares us. Sometime we might not find you. Then how do you think we'd feel?"

"You really get scared?"

Gus behaved himself for the rest of their tour.

That evening in their family room, after Gus had been put to bed, Mrs. Howard said, "Look at this pile of writing. And by a six-year-old! Hugh, you'll have to read these stories Gus wrote."

Nick looked away from the TV. "Yeah, he says they're the best in the class. Must be great to have all that confidence." At least I'm not as bad as I was, he thought. Mrs. Pope had written "Coming right along, Nicholas!" on his last paper.

Nick and Marty watched TV; Mr. Howard read the *Telegraph*; and Mrs. Howard read Gus's stories for several peaceful minutes. And then Mrs. Howard coughed, loudly and deliberately.

"Listen to this one. 'How to Raze a Hegghog. First, you find a hegghog in yor gardin. Treet it nice and it will luv you. Give it milk and leftovurs. Let it run arownd yor room. Give it pardees with othur hegghog frends. Pet it frunt to back so its qwils wont pook you. Take good care of yor hegghog.' "

Nick and Marty did not look at each other. Mr. Howard leaned his head back and roared with laughter.

"Boys," said their mother, "I feel sure you have something to tell me."

Nick glanced from under lowered eyelids to see how Marty was taking this. After all, he had found the hedgehogs.

"Okay, you got us," Marty said philosophically. "They want to hibernate anyway. They're in our closets. We'll put them back in the garden tomorrow."

"In your closets?" Mrs. Howard yelped. "And I didn't know? How long?"

"Since September," Nick said. "They've been real happy. They just sleep all day anyway. Want to see one?"

Mr. Howard wiped tears of laughter off his face. "All of them," he said. "Let's see them all."

Nick and Marty brought down Spike, Pokey, and Mrs. Tiggy-Winkle. Gus hadn't even stirred in bed when they'd removed his squeaking pet from his closet.

Three spiny balls sat in a clump on the family-room floor. Every now and then the ball that was Mrs. Tiggy-Winkle went *"Eeee."*

"Poor things," crooned Mrs. Howard. "They're scared to death. Let's put them back now, okay?"

Spike uncurled and raised his snout in the air, eyes closed. He yawned, belched, and put his head back down. He swayed sleepily, but didn't move.

"Sort of boring pets, aren't they?" Mr. Howard asked. "Last fall, when I said to put out bowls of milk, I meant we'd feed them in the garden, not drag them inside."

Nick sighed. "They're more fun inside." He stroked Spike's quills till they lay down. Spike stretched out, snoring, on the floor beside Nick's leg.

Pokey and Mrs. Tiggy-Winkle remained obstinately curled up. Marty picked them up and cradled them in his arms. "Come on, Nick. They know it's winter. We can make nests for them tomorrow in the hay out back."

Nick carried Spike upstairs and tucked him in his closet nest for the last time. "Spike, you heard what we said. You'll have to go back to the garden. Maybe you'd rather do that, huh?"

There was no response from Spike, no little whiffle or grunt, and Nick sadly shut the closet

157

door. He told himself he'd get busy and forget about his hedgehog—especially after Spike was back outside—but he knew better.

The next day was Sunday. Nick played scrum half for the Baggsley Under-Twelves for the last half of the game. They were tied 4–4 with Esher when Nick went in. He made several good passes and caught a few, but Baggsley couldn't score. Esher's boys were big, and good at knocking their opponents into the mud.

In the scrum, Diggery said, "Look, Nick, get the ball, give it to me, and just get yourself down there. We'll work it your way, see? Like Wednesday in practice, remember?"

He remembered. When the ball shot out of the scrum, he handed it off to Diggery and started running. Diggery and the tall kid from South London passed back and forth as the Baggsley team zigzagged down the field.

Nick hopped up and down about ten yards from the goal. He darted out to the center, caught the pass from South London, and headed for the goal. Esher's forwards came pounding at him. Nick dodged one but slammed into another. He lurched sideways and kept on going, right across the goal line. He touched the ball down just as Diggery and South London piled on top of him, whooping joyously. Baggsley held the score and Nick rode home a hero.

At home, stripping off his rugby kit in the laundry room, Nick knew what he had to do next . . . help Marty and Gus put their pets back in the garden. Up, down, up, down, Nick thought as he ran water into the laundry sink. One minute things are great, the next minute they stink. Why can't anything stay the same for once?

He began to feel better as he tucked Spike into his hay nest behind the garden hedge. Spike sniffed his new home with its leaves and grasses that Marty had said were "realistic," and snuggled down with a happy grunt. Nick could hear him snoring as he stood there. "It's better for you here," Nick told him, and he believed it now.

About a week later, all the family drove to Heathrow to meet Jut. Nick's mom made them sing "Frère Jacques" and "Alouette" on the way so that she could practice her French pronunciation. At Easter, they were all going to Paris, where Mr. Howard had a business meeting. People in England traveled to France the way

Americans visited a neighboring state. It was less than an hour by plane.

"I'm going to learn French if it kills me," Mrs. Howard had announced. "Everyone I meet over here speaks at least two languages. It's humiliating!"

"*Le français est facile*," Marty had told her.

"He means French is easy," Nick translated. "It isn't as bad as I thought. Just say everything way back in your throat or up in your nose." Nick had borrowed one of the tapes from his school language lab for his mother to use.

Now, while everyone was singing in French, Nick thought about the family trip to Paris. And the other one to Switzerland. While I'm in Ohio, he said to himself.

And where will I live? Nick had avoided asking himself this question all fall. Now, he imagined his friends' homes and discarded them one by one. He wasn't sure he could live at Bobby's. Once, yes. But things had changed. He hadn't even thought of Bobby since Thanksgiving.

Jut's plane was on time and he was as excited as everyone else. "Hey, some wheels!" he said as they got ready to drive home. He stroked the cherry-red paint on the Volvo wagon.

"We only need one car here," his father said, "so we splurged. I'll take you home, Jut, but then I have to go to work. Have you grown, son?"

"About an inch. I need new shoes. And Mom, can you let down my suit pants?"

"The brand-new ones?"

"Yup. I look like I'm expecting a flood."

His dad smiled. "Some things never change."

Marty and Nick promised to show Jut where the hedgehogs wintered in the hay behind the hedge. Gus made him promise to read his stories. Mrs. Howard said, "We all sure missed you, Jut. Every day."

"He's home now," Nick said.

Jut leaned toward Nick. "So now it's home, huh?"

Nick just frowned and said nothing.

Jut started to speak, but stopped when he saw Nick's face. "We'll talk later," he said quietly.

They drove down Kings' Ride and turned into the driveway. "Whooee! Just like you said. Right out of a book, Mom. Thatched roof and all."

"It's over two hundred years old," she replied.

"So's the plumbing," Nick added. "Don't drink the water upstairs. And pull the chains in the loo twice."

16

For the next week, while Nick, Marty, and Gus went to school, Mrs. Howard took Jut to see the sights. Nick spent most afternoons at school, practicing for the big Christmas program. Twice he had evening rehearsals.

"You sure don't have to worry about being bored over here," Jut told Nick and Marty one night. "Mom's wearing me out."

"This play's wearing me out." Nick pillowed his head on his arms. They were all in his room, and he had stretched out on the bed. "We've got only a week of rehearsals left, but I think it's going to be great."

"You guys are coming to Oxford with us tomorrow, aren't you?" Jut asked. "Sight-seeing's okay, but when I'm alone with Mom, I can't get her to *leave* anyplace! She should just pitch a tent in Trafalgar Square and be done with it."

Nick and Marty grinned at each other.

The next morning, all the Howards except Gus headed north for Oxford. Gus was staying with his friend Robert.

" 'Bye, Gus. See you tonight," Mrs. Howard called from the car as Gus charged up Robert's sidewalk. As they drove away she said. "He'd have hated this trip, and Robert's mum loves children."

"Robert's mum," mimicked Jut. "You wouldn't believe how the vocabulary of this family has changed in four months!"

His dad chuckled. "We're around British people all day, and it's catching. I always say *loo* now, and *dustbin*, and *gammon* for ham—that's an odd one for Americans—and *lorry* for this blasted truck that's in my way!"

"He's become a regular Grand Prix driver," Jut said, as if his father weren't in the car.

"Hey, kid, whose side are you on? Look at

these roads! We don't have two roads this smooth in the whole state of Ohio!" Mr. Howard zoomed around the lorry.

Nick enjoyed the famous colleges of Oxford because Jut was with them. On their guided tour, Jut spoke with two students who later showed them their rooms and their eating hall, a magnificent, wood-paneled beauty over five hundred years old.

When they went to the brass-rubbing center, Jut and Nick worked together rubbing the tall brass of a long-dead knight.

"When I give this to Gwen, she is going to flip out," Jut said. He rubbed his gold wax crayon carefully over the thin black paper taped on top of the brass.

Mr. and Mrs. Howard and Marty each did a separate rubbing, in black crayon on white paper. They planned to frame theirs for the front hall. "I might get a special insurance policy on these things," Mr. Howard joked. "This is trickier than it looks."

Nick and Jut rubbed in companionable silence, moving their crayons back and forth repeatedly on each segment of their knight to get an even coating of gold. "You want to tell me about school?" Jut asked after a time.

Nick began to talk about school, just bits at first, then more. He talked about Diggery. He explained how Nigel felt about Akbar and why he had joined Scouts. He tried to explain rugby. "We have a big game tomorrow. You'll come, won't you?"

"Will it rain?"

"Does the Queen have a crown?"

"Yuk, yuk, very funny. Have you guys noticed that the Queen, or somebody royal, is on the front page of the English newspapers almost *every day*?" Jut carefully outlined his knight's long sword.

"Royalty's a big deal here, Jut. It's not like home. It's not like home at all."

"But you're handling it, Nick. And so's Marty. I can't get over how you zip around on the trains—into London—into Windsor—just like you've been here forever."

"The trains are great! But we won't zip into London if the IRA keeps threatening. They give bombs for Christmas. They love crowds."

"Whooeee," Jut breathed. "That's heavy."

"Yeah, but we just pay attention in places like London or train stations. Mom's uptight, though."

"We don't hear much about this in America," Jut said.

Nick thought a moment before he spoke. "It's too far away, I guess. We're *very far away*, Jut. I thought so, that first night in the airport, but now I know for sure. It's not just words, like *lorry* and *loo*, it's everything. Holidays, and traditions, and schools, and history—this place is stuffed with history! And they know about war and we don't—not really. It's all different."

Jut looked up from the rubbing. "One thing sure is different. You and Marty don't fight all the time. And if I hadn't known who was talking just now I'd say the guy was about sixteen. I'm impressed, Nick. . . . I mean that."

Nick didn't know what to say. If he sounded about sixteen, like Jut said, then why had tears come to his eyes? Was he going to boo-hoo just because his brother had praised him?

"Thanks" was all he could manage. He kept his eyes on the rubbing until he thought of something else to say.

"Wait till you meet Marty's friends," Nick said. "Some boarders we know—Rajeev and Mufu— are coming for dinner before they go home on holiday. They're a blast!"

Jut put his crayon down to flex his fingers. "But you have Diggery . . . and Akbar. And your rugby team and Scouts. You're handling it, Nick, like I said."

Nick was silent as he crayoned the faithful dog at the knight's feet. He rubbed the gold wax along the dog's outline and didn't slip off the edge of the raised brass even on the slender tail.

Jut bent over Nick's work. "When did you become such an artist?"

"Since I met Mrs. Pope," Nick answered grimly.

"Oh, yeah, the one who likes full stops." Jut grinned. "Tell me more about school, Nick. And about your trip to Wales, especially those twenty miles in the rain. I want to know everything."

"Everything?"

"Let 'er rip," Jut said, picking up his crayon.

In the next few days, Nick had almost no time to spend with Jut. Most afternoons and evenings he was in rehearsals for the Christmas production. Until now, practices had been fairly relaxed. As the last days flew by, everyone became nervous and excited about the upcoming performance.

"No, no, no!" Mrs. Pope shouted in dress rehearsal. "You lot can't crowd through the doorway! This is a procession to set the scene and give everyone a chance to see your costumes. You're processing regally into the castle courtyard. *Regally*, mind! You, David, you're a monk. Cast your eyes down and look humble and stop twitching at your robe!"

"It itches somethin' awww-ful," David complained, writhing under the brown homespun of his monk's habit.

Nick, in full armor for the first time, forced up the visor of his helmet, which shrieked in protest.

Mrs. Pope whirled round. "What was that?"

"My helmet. I don't think this visor's been raised in six centuries," Nick explained.

The class giggled, and even Mrs. Pope relaxed enough to smile. "We'll give it a drop of oil. It has to go up and down, and we can't have it squeaking like that."

She turned back to the crowd jammed in the doorway. Akbar tested his helmet, which was quiet, and said to Nick, "I am glad these clothings are gone. Since today, I think knight's clothings are terrible. Mine hurts everywhere."

"It's miserable, all right." Nick spread his feet

apart, which was the only way he could bear to stand. "But our joust is the big deal, and we don't have a ton of lines."

Akbar grinned. "That is because we are the best at the drama, Nick. We would shame the others, is it not so?"

"Right!" Nick said. "We'd better practice getting on and off our horses. It was okay when we just had the chain mail, but in these metal suits, I don't know."

While the rest of the class tried to process more regally, Nick and Akbar rounded up their horses. As knights in the joust, they were to appear last, after the rest of the cast had gathered in the courtyard onstage.

Nick's horse was Diggery and Nigel in a black horse costume that had a hardboard seat underneath for Nick to sit on. Diggery was the head of the horse. "Stand still," Nick told his horse, which was pawing the gym floor and whinnying.

"Right, mate," said the horse's head. "Don't just climb on, then. You're a knight. Leap on, see what I mean?"

"You're crazy, but I'll try it," Nick agreed. He stepped back a few feet to get a run at his horse. Armor clanking, he threw himself up onto its back. He slid right off the other side and crashed to the floor.

The horse howled with laughter. Nick picked himself up awkwardly and went to the horse's head. "I knew you were crazy," he said. "That horse material is too slippery. It'd be different if we had a saddle."

"No saddle, mate," said the horse's rear end. "They're too heavy. That's why the saddle's painted on the material."

"It's too slippery!" Nick yelled.

"This idea is not good," observed Akbar. "We come in on the horses. We stay on for the joust. After, we get off. We must practice getting off."

"Knights?" called Mrs. Pope. "We're ready for the knights now! Remember, you're to charge through the doorway, across the back of the room, and down to the center aisle. Sit erectly, please, so that you look proud and haughty!

"Sir Hubert, you come first, then Sir Percival. Shoulders back, lances straight up in the air, visors down!"

Nick was Sir Hubert. He forced the squeaking visor down into place and clambered aboard his black horse.

"Charge!" Diggery hissed to Nigel at the rear.

Nick rode, swaying dangerously, as they tried to gallop past the last row of seats. "Not so jerky!" he begged.

The horse galloped into the turn to head down the center aisle and the rear half separated. Nick slid off the middle of his horse and crashed to the floor again.

Nigel's head poked out of the horse's middle. "Not so bloomin' fast on the turn, Diggery!"

"Let's try that again!" Mrs. Pope called out.

"Oh, brother," Akbar said, cantering over to where Nick lay on the floor. "How did we get this big-deal part?"

Nick forced his visor up so that he could see Akbar. "Next time, we'll ask for lines instead, okay?"

17

Nick was too excited to eat dinner the night of the Christmas program. If I eat, I'll barf, he thought.

"If you've forgotten anything," his dad said as they got into the car, "just call home. I can bring whatever it is when I come back with the rest of the family."

Nick thought he had everything. His lance, made from a broomstick painted silver, was in the backseat with his chain mail. He looked out the window, seeing nothing, saying his few lines over and over to himself.

After several blocks he said, "I just wish we didn't have to ride those dumb horses."

"Sounds tricky, all right, but very authentic—much more elaborate than any play I was in as a kid."

"Don't remind me," Nick said weakly. "Just be on time, okay? I'll write your names on the programs on your seats."

At school, Nick lined up with the rest of the cast waiting to be made up. Akbar stepped back in line to stand beside him. They were dressed alike in black leotards, over which they wore the silvery chain mail. They had made their silver, metal-looking footgear out of cardboard covered with foil.

"Stand still, lad," said Mrs. Mitchell, the makeup lady. Nick had never felt so jittery. He jumped back when she dabbed the red dot in the corner of each eye.

When she finished, Nick looked at himself in a mirror. His eyes, already large and dark, looked huge now. His cheeks were blushed with pink, his lips darkened slightly. Lines of age marked his face below the silvered, dark hair. Yeah, I look just right, he thought.

At the last minute, he and Akbar got into their suits of armor. The gym had filled with family and guests by then. Two rooms away,

Nick heard their chatter, and his jitters turned into a stomachache. He went to talk to his horse.

"Hey, Diggery, Nigel—it's me, Nick."

"Ay, your lordship?" The horse's rear end giggled.

Nick clenched his metal fists. "Nigel!" he hissed, where he thought Nigel's head would be. "If you guys mess up like you did in practice, we're going to look like idiots!"

"Relax, mate," said the horse's head. "You hear him, Nigel. He *means* it. Now I'm not goin' round the turn so fast, so you *hang on!* You're the one who said we had to be the horse, remember?"

"Awwl right," Nigel grumbled. "Funnier the other way."

"We're not supposed to be funny!" Nick said desperately. "We're supposed to be tense and exciting!"

The school orchestra began the overture of Christmas music, and Mrs. Pope shut the door to their room.

"Silence," she whispered. "It won't be long now."

Nick leaned against the wall and mumbled his lines. Akbar clanked up beside him. "The music is very beautiful," he said, sighing. "Next time, I shall play in the orchestra."

Finally, it was time for the fourth-years' sketch. On tiptoe, they moved down the hall toward the gym.

The king, played by Frederick, who was tall and blond, strode regally into the gym at the head of the procession. On his arm was the queen, played by auburn-haired Fiona. The orchestra piped a delicate air for flutes and recorders as court attendants in medieval costumes followed the monarchs. One court jester juggled three gold balls as he went along; another did somersaults. Four monks paced solemnly in line. Scullery maids and cooks, pages, groomsmen, and stable boys marched behind, each carrying a prop for use in their sketch.

When they had paraded across the back of the gym and down the far side, they took their places onstage in the castle courtyard. The castle, an impressive monument of wood and cardboard, formed the background.

The king bowed his queen to her seat under a satin canopy and sat beside her to watch the entertainment. Both court jesters juggled balls, then rings. They did several tumbling tricks before walking across the stage on their hands while playing harmonicas.

Five ladies of the court came forth to strum lutes and sing "Greensleeves" with orchestra accompaniment.

The scullery maids and cooks bustled about at one side of the stage, setting out a long table of food for the royal feast. The monks clustered around the table and gazed hungrily at each new dish.

"Ho, there, Friar Lackaday!" the king called. "Have you and your brothers entertainment to earn your bread this day?"

"Oh, yes, your highness," Friar Lackaday said, with a lingering glance for the table. "We have a new riddle for ye who are so fond of riddles."

The four monks grouped before the throne. Taking turns, line by line, they recited:

"A moth ate a word."

"When I learned of that wonder, it seemed to me strange that a worm would devour the words of a man."

"That a thief in the night would eat the speech of the great as well as the book that held them."

"Nor was that stealthy visitor made any wiser by those words that he consumed."

Friar Lackaday, who was David and still itching in his monk's robe, looked slyly at the king.

"Can you guess it, your majesty?"

The king conferred with his queen. "I think we have foiled you once again, good brother. The queen and I say it is a *bookworm!*"

Friar Lackaday nodded, downcast. "Ah, your majesties are too clever by half." He turned to his fellow monks. "We shall have to get up pretty early in the morning to fool this pair, brothers."

At this the audience laughed, and the king and queen smiled complacently. Friar Lackaday and his brothers resumed their watch by the table.

TA DA DEE DA DEE DAAA! blared two pages with trumpets.

"Your majesty, horsemen approach!" said one page.

This was it. Nick clamped his legs around his steed and whispered, "Hurry—but not too fast! Remember the corner!"

Nick sat as straight as he could, lance erect, visor down. His steed charged, whinnying, across the back of the gym. At the corner, the black horse slowed and lumbered into the turn. Nick didn't care if it looked awkward. It was better than crashing to the floor.

His horse picked up speed as he thundered

down the center aisle and up the ramp onto the stage.

Akbar pounded right behind him on a white horse. Onstage, both horses stopped abruptly, snorted, and pawed the ground just inches in front of the thrones.

"Your majesties," Nick said, removing this helmet.

"Your majesties," echoed Akbar.

"What say you, Sir Hubert? Who is this strange knight that comes after you?" the king demanded.

"He be Sir Percival, a man of no honor," Nick said, praying that he sounded angry and forceful.

The king leaned toward Sir Percival. "What say you to this charge, Sir Percival?"

"It is false!" Akbar then removed his helmet. "He has refused me the hand of his daughter, the beautiful Lady Elizabeth. I have come to prove that I am worthy."

The king inclined his head. "So be it." He waved grandly to the servants. "Clear the way!" To the knights he said, "There will be no deaths today. Our entertainment is in honor of the queen's birthday, and so I order you to blunt your lances. The queen will determine the winner. Now, let the joust begin!"

TA DA DEE DA DEE DAAA! blared the trumpets again.

Sir Hubert spurred his steed, and it said, "Not so, 'ard, mate, we're goin'!"

Sir Hubert readied his tilting lance and charged from stage left toward the center, straight at Sir Percival. Hooves thundered across the stage. As they passed, Sir Hubert landed a glancing blow on Sir Percival's shoulder, but both knights stayed in the saddle.

They braked at the end of the run and turned, their horses pawing the ground before charging again. This time Sir Hubert's blow sent Sir Percival crashing to the ground in a clatter of metal.

Sir Percival heaved himself up, felt of his chest, and turned to shake a fist at Sir Hubert. "A lucky blow!" he cried. "We shall see who lands the next!" He climbed back onto his horse and prepared to charge again.

Again they hurtled toward one another. Sir Percival's lance jabbed into Sir Hubert's stomach. He swayed dangerously, touching the ground with one hand, then righted himself and finished the run erect.

Once more they turned, and Sir Hubert cried, "Yield, dog! I cannot be unhorsed by a mere youth!"

"Charge!" cried Sir Percival, his lance pointing at Sir Hubert's heart as he galloped straight for him.

Sir Hubert pounded toward his enemy. *Thwack!* Down went Sir Hubert and down went his horse.

The queen leaped to her feet. "Cease!" she cried, flapping a length of silk in the air, "Sir Hubert, I find that you are *both* worthy knights. But, as a birthday favor, I beg you to allow Sir Percival to wed your daughter."

Sir Hubert stood up and helped his horse to assemble itself. He removed his helmet and bowed toward the queen. "It shall be as you wish, your highness."

The king leaped to his feet. "Splendid! Let us celebrate with a dance before the feast. Music!" he commanded, pointing to the orchestra.

All onstage took their positions for the dance, an intricate series of steps and bowings that they had practiced with the games mistress for weeks. The costumed figures swirled to and fro while the orchestra played a haunting fourteenth-century melody. The finale was an elaborate bow to the audience.

The audience went crazy. Older brothers whistled; other kids shouted "Bravo!"; then parents began to stand up. And the clapping didn't stop. The cast bowed again, and then again. The orchestra stood and bowed too.

Nick glowed inside. They had done well. Better than well. They were fantastic! He heard the special, piercing whistle Jut saved for football games. He could see his dad holding Gus up in the air. Gus was yelling, of course.

The curtain dropped and Mrs. Pope dashed onto the stage. "You were fantastic!" she told them. "Everything was just perfect! Now, run along to your parents. They can pick you up after the cast party, about eleven I should think. I'll go help to lay on the party."

"Terrific, Nick!" Jut said, when they met in the hall.

"Sure looked like fun," added Marty, grinning.

"Best play we ever saw!" said Mrs. Howard. "It had everything—funny parts, and beautiful parts, and the joust was really exciting. No wonder you practiced so many times!"

"This was the best we ever did it," Nick said. "It's the horses, really. They have the tough part."

"I wanta wear this armor sometime," Gus said, touching the metal parts on Nick's costume.

Mr. Howard bowed. "Sir Hubert, O worthy knight, when wouldst thou I return with thy chariot?"

"Not till eleven, Dad. They're laying on a great party and I'm starving."

"Laying it on?" Jut asked.

"That's the way we say it, mate. See you later." Nick waved good-bye and clanked down to the dressing room.

He and Akbar, divested of their metal, joined the party, and Nick went to find his horse. "Hey, you guys were awesome!"

Diggery and Nigel, mouths full of food, nodded happily. "We got the feel of it this time, you know?" Diggery said. "We were together, like a real horse and rider. Wish we could do it again. I like whinnying."

"I wanted to try rearin' up, see? Like a proper horse, only Diggery said you'd fall off."

"Pity we can't do it again," Diggery repeated. "We made a great team. Akbar and his horse, as well."

Frederick, in kingly robes minus the crown, came over to talk. "Hey, Nick, Abkar, you lot were brilliant! Smashing falls. How'd you make it look so real?"

"It is much skill with the drama," Akbar said. "You have seen this in class, right?"

"Oh, right!" Frederick grinned and held out a plate. "Here, try these. They're little pizzas. Really smashing."

Nick ate six of the pizzas and at least six of everything else. They all talked about doing the play again.

"I'll speak to the headmaster," Mrs. Pope promised. "Maybe we could give it again, our last afternoon next week. The First School would come, I'm sure, and maybe Windsor Middle School. That would be fun, wouldn't it?"

The boys who'd been the white horse began discussing horse behavior with the black horse. Both wanted to try rearing up in the air before their next performance.

"Oh, brother," Akbar said to Nick. "The horses are getting uppity. They must be put in the stable."

Nick, Diggery, Nigel, and the boys who had played the white horse were convulsed with laughter. "Where'd you learn 'uppity'?" Nick asked when he could talk.

"John Wayne. Best of the American actors."

"Right!" Diggery and Nigel chorused.

David and James brought their lemonade and cake and sat down with Nick, Akbar, and the two horses. "You looked like real knights," David said. "Smashing falls!"

Sometime in the middle of the cast party— when the food was gone and they were still happily congratulating one another—Nick knew that he belonged. He was part of this class. He liked sitting next to Akbar every day in school. Of course, the Christmas program had helped. But maybe he'd just been here long enough.

And he belonged to the rugby team, too. After one Sunday when his mom had kept him home with a cold, Coach Stewart had said, "Och, we missed ye, lad! A tie game we had without ye. And all the lads wonderin' where ye were." He had scratched his head in a distracted manner.

Nick had explained about his cold and his mother.

"Well, then, that's the way of it. I just wanted ye to know we depend on ye, Nicholas."

And there were Scout trips still to come. They

185

were so grueling that they'd be called "wilderness training" at home, he thought, amused.

There were BMX trails he had yet to ride, but which Diggery had lovingly described. And the family trips to Switzerland and Paris—and maybe other neat places.

I can't go back home, he told himself as he got into bed that night—not yet anyway. He thought of Spike, who was part of the garden, whose home *had* to be in the garden. "But I'm not like that," he said out loud.

He remembered the time in August when he'd been starving himself so they'd send him back to Ohio—where he thought he belonged. In the dark of his room, he grinned.

I guess I am stubborn. . . . But England must be stubborner, he decided. As he burrowed contentedly under the covers, Nick heard again the dependable rattle of the train pulling into Baggsley-on-Thames.